Stuart Hood was born in Scotland in 1915 and educated at Edinburgh University. He has written several novels (*The Circle of the Minotaur, Since the Fall, In and Out the Window* and *The Upper Hand*) as well as books on television (*A Survey of Television, Radio and Television, On Television*). He was head of the BBC World Service and Controller of Programmes at BBC Television. He is currently a freelance producer of TV documentaries and a script-writer for the BBC and ITV. He is also a prolific translator.

STUART HOOD

A Storm from Paradise

PALADIN
GRAFTON BOOKS
A Division of the Collins Publishing Group

LONDON GLASGOW
TORONTO SYDNEY AUCKLAND

Paladin
Grafton Books
A Division of the Collins Publishing Group
8 Grafton Street, London W1X 3LA

Published by Paladin Books
in association with Carcanet 1988

First published in Great Britain by
Carcanet Press Ltd 1985

Copyright © Stuart Hood 1985

ISBN 0-586-08716-8

Printed and bound in Great Britain by
Collins, Glasgow

Set in Bembo

This is how one perceives the angel of history. His face is turned towards the past. Where we perceive a chain of events he sees one single catastrophe. . . . The angel would like to stay, awaken the dead, and make whole what has been smashed. But a storm is blowing from Paradise, it has got caught in his wings with such violence that the angel can no longer close them . . . This storm is what we call progress.

WALTER BENJAMIN: *Theses on the philosophy of history*

Usually for picnics we took a small brake seating about eight people. It was my ambition and privilege, established by my mother, to sit by the coachman with his rug over my knees, watching the rolling motion of the horse's rump and seeing with fascination the way it defecated, spilling the yellow dung in little balls that dropped out of sight between the wheels. Meantime the ladies in the back sat with their feet on the picnic hampers, talking and laughing and pretending not to notice the smell when the horse farted. The men scouted ahead on their bicycles or, on the hills, came alongside to be pulled up the gradients. There were two main picnic places — one on the West Water and the other on the East Water. Of these I preferred the latter, for after the farm at Dalbog with its Druid's stones the road stopped, the coachman clambered down and opened a gate on to a rutted track across the moors. As we passed, we put up whirring coveys of grouse and startled the black-faced sheep with their sweeping horns and tangled pelts. The ground rose gently to a point where the driver would stop to allow the cyclists to catch up, for they found it hard going on the rough and narrow track. As we waited, I would climb down to find in the bank above the road a spring of clear cold water with a taste of peat. In front of us the valley of the East Water narrowed between bare hills — sheep-runs of heather and grass; within the sheltered re-entrants, broom and gorse. The trees were small: alder and birch with here and there at the side of a ruined cottage or by a sheep-fold a mountain ash, a rowan, set there to shield the occupants from evil spirits and witches. From the spring the road dropped slowly down to a confluence of the waters where the burn joined the East

Water. They met beyond a stone bridge built to allow the gentlemen from London and America and the dark-skinned princes from India to drive as close to the butts as possible when the grouse-shooting season opened in August. The Mooran Burn ran through a dark overgrown ravine. Below the bridge it joined the river which here was caught in deep amber-coloured pools separated by little rapids and falls. Beyond the bridge and to the right was (is) a long triangle of grass on which we would picnic. A fire was started in a hearth formed from three large stones and the kettle set to boil on top. Rugs were shaken out, table cloths spread, and all my mother's baking unpacked: scones, pancakes, sponges, seed-cakes, buns. When the first food was laid out the wasps and flies were already there along with clouds of midges from the little pools of stagnant water where the ground turned marshy. The horse, freed from the brake which stood on the road by the bridge with its shafts rising high in the air, whisked at the insects with its tail and shook its head in its nose-bag. The driver smoked a pipe a little apart, for he knew his place. After the meal there were games of rounders in which everyone joined except the oldest and most serious members of the party — the minister, for instance, who had never been known to run. The women as they ran gathered up their skirts with one hand or else held their hats on their heads and everyone laughed a great deal. Some of the men would have rods and move off up the Burn to find the pools where the trout lay, one in each hillside pool and difficult to get at because of the overhanging hazels or birches. Others clambered on to the rocks that held the pools of the East Water and cast their flies into the tail of the runs where the river brimmed over in abrupt rapids. Groups of two or three explored the riverside — women and children, young girls, couples moving away from the hearth, talking and laughing and throwing stones into the pools to the annoyance of the fishers. If the weather held — if there was no mountain thunderburst to bring the Burn down in a sudden wall of water and to send the company running for shelter among the trees or under an overhanging rock — it would be evening before the coachman, pulling out his plump silver watch, gave the sign for return by leading his horse up to the road and backing it in between the shafts. On the way back once a great tawny owl watched us from a fence post then, as we drew almost abreast, rose and flew off silently with quick powerful strokes of its wings. If the fishers had been lucky there might be when we got home a sink full of brown trout in the scullery: beautiful, slippery and cold.

I imagine that it was on one such outing — the annual choir outing, perhaps — that John Scott first met, first found himself in the company of the organist, Miss May Mitchell, who was to be my mother. He must have known her of course, have greeted her when she came up the steps of the church with her music-case — always the first to arrive — for as newly appointed head of the village school he had felt obliged to accept the duties of elder and treasurer of the Free Kirk. From his pew, he saw mostly her back and her reddish hair which, as she played, tended to come loose and slip down on to her shoulders. He came to know the gesture with which at the end of a hymn or psalm or paraphrase she would readjust it, tucking it up under her hat and replacing her hat-pin. During the sermon she left her organ stool and went to sit in a pew at the very front of the congregation along with her father, the owner of the wool mill, her mother, her sister Euphemia and her brother Jim, who had left the village school and now travelled daily to the grammar school fifteen miles down the line in a seaside town which boasted that its Academy had been the first school in Scotland to teach ancient Greek. It was to talk about Jim that she approached him during the choir outing, I expect, climbing out to where he sat on a boulder and idly threw twigs and pieces of driftwood into the pool below to see how they were caught and held by the eddies and drawn into the side of the rocks among the thick yellow foam from the falls. Jim was having trouble with his French and his maths, she said, could he help? They heard he had lived a while in France and must fairly speak like the French themselves. Would he be prepared to coach Jim — for a fee naturally. Her father had asked her to approach him and would be most beholden to him if he agreed. Which he did readily, not — as she suggested — out of kindness or at this moment because of any attraction he felt in her, but because he was bored and starved of company. And it would be a chance to brush up his own French grammar. Jim was, he suspected, a poor plodding pupil in French though bright enough, no doubt, where internal combustion engines were concerned and always hanging about the stables by the station where the proprietor had acquired a motor-car, a De Dion Bouton. His ambition, his sister said, was to own a motorcycle but his father had made it a condition that he pass his exams and finish his education.

This, as I surmise, is how they came to know each other for they were never — either of them — explicit to their children about how it had happened or how their acquaintance had ripened into courtship. Naturally they did not admit to us that there had been a hiatus in their relationship — a breach healed only with difficulty and because of parental and social pressures. However that may be, shortly after the outing he made his first visit to the mill on his bicycle, which had arrived by goods train — a stout model with a freewheel mechanism and a three-speed gear. For dark nights there was an acetylene lamp to fit on a bracket on the handlebars; a drip of water on to the chemical set off a gas (C_2H_2) that burned with a steady flame and gave off a slightly pungent smell. His way to the mill took him over the High Street, past the end of the smithy and down the hill by the side of the gasworks — 'the gassy brae' — that led to the East Water. There a path turned off to the left, rising sharply over a sandstone bluff, past clumps of ash and blackthorn, to the suspension bridge where care had to be taken not to get the front tyre jammed in the gaps between the planks underfoot. As he crossed, the whole structure swayed gently above the water which, having run dark and deep to beneath the bridge now shallowed over shelving stretches of sandstone to widen out into broken rapids in a bend beneath high sandstone cliffs. Once over the bridge the road turned right along the lade by a narrow road, in summer cool and odorous with crushed herbs. Then past the cartway to the ford where the high-stepping Clydesdale horses plunged in and fronted the current as they pulled their high-carts across with the great wheels up to the hub in the water. Not far beyond the ford was the miller's house — a long whitewashed building with outhouses that made a rectangle round a stretch of grass and a border of flowers. Below the house, sloping down to the river, was an apple orchard where the bees drifted in and out of the skeps — their wicker hives. The lade ran in its channel along the crest of the hill and on to the mill, which was built on the side of a slope so that the water fell powerfully on the blades of the water-wheel. Inside the mill the owner ruled among the clamour of the machinery and the click of the shuttles as they wove the tweeds, the blankets and the rugs, and the stout cloth that covered the backs of the farmers in the parish and had even been used by the local tailor to cut a shooting jacket for Major MacIllroy of the Burnfoot. The owner, Mr Mitchell, was a tall taciturn man with a long beard behind which he concealed his feelings, his emotions and moods. He was dusty from the mill, kind to children in a curious silent way that placed them on the same level as a puppy-dog or a pony.

When last I went that way fifteen years or so ago the house and the mill were gone and the trees in the orchard had been cleared. I had intended to walk past the mill to see whether there was still a bank where the primroses and violets came early every spring. But it started to rain and I turned back to my hotel.

Mrs Mitchell was a tiny woman with a dark vivacious face. She came from the Black Isle and still had a strong Highland accent which embarrassed her family except for Jim, who found ways to make her say jam or jug or junction, knowing that they would be transformed — if she was not paying attention — to cham, chug and chunction. Her father, a small farmer, had died young leaving a large family; the daughters went into service or found work as nannies — which was perhaps how she met Mr Mitchell when he visited one of the big houses in the county to show his wares. In the low-roofed kitchen and the adjoining dining-room (used only rarely) she imposed a standard of cleanliness — having herself been brought up in a hard school — that was famous in the village and in the cottar-houses from which she drew her serving-girls. They came straight from school at thirteen and learned to cook, to clean, to polish, to starch and iron; it was a grand training, she used to say, and lamented that they never stayed. For that she did not dream, in her blind affection, of blaming Jim who would catch the girls in dark corners and try to snatch kisses or to bribe them 'to let him see'. So they would leave her and some big house or some manse gladly took them in.

If she was indulgent with her son, with her daughters she was a martinet. The younger, Euphemia — Phemy — had perfected stratagems for escaping from her mother's discipline and from the needlework, knitting, embroidery, cooking and piano practice, by casting herself as 'the delicate one'. In this role she was mysterious and elusive, spending long hours in her bedroom from which she emerged looking pale and per-versely thin, for although she ate she could keep nothing down — a condition for which the doctor prescribed an invalid diet of egg-custards, brains, thin oatmeal gruel, calves' foot jelly and boiled chicken. It did nothing to plump out her skinny arms and barely developed breasts. There were other more mysterious aspects of her condition to which her mother referred by elaborate indirections but which gossip suc-cinctly defined by asserting that she wasn't a woman yet. May, the organist, the one who was to be my mother, was — as her father sometimes put it with a certain understanding that bordered on affection — the Martha of the household. She was quiet, industrious, well-behaved and capable at whatever job she undertook, whether it was hanging out the sheets or playing the organ. Beneath it all, I believe, she was furiously resentful of her mother's regime and her sister's invalid fads, She herself was up early to feed the hens and search for the eggs dropped in the orchard and under the hedges, carrying water from the pump that was their only supply and chasing Jim off

12

to catch the eight o'clock train to school. On Mondays she helped with the washing, which in summer was spread on the grass under the apple trees and hurriedly scooped into a washing basket if a visitor like the headmaster arrived. On Tuesday there was ironing and darning. On Wednesday she was in the village for organ practice and evening choir practice having had to rout out the reluctant ones from their homes and get them through the psalms and hymns. There was no time here for elaborate descant or faux-bourdon: it was enough if they kept to their parts and if the bass, who farmed at the end of the village, did not suddenly rise to the same fortissimo with which he called in his collie dog and drown the thin voices of the sopranos. She was, beneath her apparent acquiescence in this routine, in a rebellious mood and eager for escape; which her father recognized, saying through his beard as he settled down to sleep: 'Our May, now, she'll be up and away one of these days.' Mrs Mitchell said nothing, which meant she agreed.

It was no doubt with her encouragement that my father was pressed to return to the mill on other days beside Saturday. During the summer holidays, with Phemy dragging behind, he and May would walk down to the river looking for nests in the hedges, picking the globe flowers in the damp places and finding among the trees wood anemones which wilted before they could even bring them home. Once they discovered a moorhen's nest on a little island of gravel and sedge and my father waded out through the shallow water to count the speckled eggs. There was a bush of strongly scented white roses by the entrance to the house which was like a cold beacon as they walked back through the summer dusk. The apples were ripening, falling with a soft thud to be pecked by hens and ducks. Once Mr Mitchell, celebrating the sale of two bolts of cloth, brought out a bottle of mead distilled from the honey of his own bees and pressed it on my father who — his scruples overcome by assurances that it was not in the accepted sense of the word spirits — drank and on the way home fell from his bicycle and barked his knee. Now as he watched the school house rise, course upon course — the bow window of the front bedroom was already built — he felt increasingly the pressures to find a suitable wife to share it with him. People wondered if there was some young lady in Stirling. His denial was received with a polite smile. The house, the builders told him, would be ready by Michaelmas. The Reverend James Murdoch, the Free Kirk minister, hinted; his wife invited the choir to tea and asked the schoolmaster on the excuse that he was the kirk treasurer. The thought of actually having to furnish the house and of setting up a household — if only with a housekeeper — filled him with a disproportionate anxiety although he had enough laid by in the bank to do so modestly. But his real fear was the need to commit himself, to propose, to become engaged, to embark on matrimony and interrupt the celibacy which so far he had only once broken: the circumstances he wished he might forget. Everything urged him towards May but when he analysed his feelings he found them far from strong. Not that he did not find her appealing with her red hair, the coolness of her skin when his hand touched her arm as he helped over a stile or a bank and the soft movement of her breasts under her dress. Once, running towards the river, both slipped on the damp red soil and landed on top of each other so that he felt her body and legs distinctly before she scrambled to her feet and, between laughter and annoyance, pointed to the red patches on her dress and on his trousers. When they got back Jim sniggered and said somethings about 'coortin' couples'. Sometimes he found her mannerisms infuriating; the way she stuck out her little finger when she drank her tea, her laugh which was often falsely polite, falsely complicit — or so it seemed to him — and even the automatic way she raised her hand to adjust her hair round her ears. At other times he felt that she was a complete stranger who had somehow been thrown together with him but to whom he had nothing to say, with whom he could share nothing beyond the simple pastoral pleasures of gathering wild flowers and counting the hens' eggs. Once arriving unexpectedly he heard her voice raised in anger as he had not heard it before. It had lost its overlay of good breeding and had relapsed into thick, expressive dialect — the language of the cottar-house girls, which her mother forbade in the house. With the vocabulary of the ploughmen's daughters, of the ploughmen themselves, she abused her sister as a thowless bizzem wi' nae spunk in her, ower finnicky to file her hands, aye poorly, a lazy bitch there was naething the matter wi' — naething that a skelpt airse wouldnae mend. And she'd dae it hersel' if naebody else wud. He drew back from the front door, slipped out into the road and appproached once more, ringing his bell loudly. 'Oh, it's you, John, fancy that now, I wasn't expecting you that soon.' She could not conceal the red flush that ran down her neck and over her chest. 'Come away in. I've been baking scones. Hot work this summer weather.'

It was probably this same summer when he was full of debates, fears and hesitations, that he took to going on long bicycle rides round Slateford. He had begun by cycling the six miles or so every other Saturday to the nearest town, where he would perhaps look into the stationer's and bookseller's to order a book; it would arrive a couple of weeks later but part of the pleasure lay in the waiting for another volume of the Waverley novels. In a sweetie shop near the ruined abbey he bought half-a-pound of boiled sweets (home-made) which he sucked on the road back up the long hill to Trinity and on past the rectangular bend where the road traced the perimeter of a northerly Roman fort. On other Saturdays his route might take him up to the Glen to the outlying castles of the Lindsays — gaunt red towers which in the fifteenth century one of the line had used, a local history said, as 'hiding holes from the inquisition made after him for his murder of a Lowland lord'. Often he took a rod with him and clambered up the side of the moorland burns, dropping his worm beyond the overhanging bank to where in the deep peaty holes the fat trout lay and gorged themselves. When he came home there might be a dozen fish in the grass-lined creel. His landlady Mrs Ramsay fried them for his supper sprinkled with oatmeal. At his invitation she sat and shared the meal.

Sometimes he cycled up the West Water to its upper reaches among bare moors. He passed lonely cottages where shepherds lived; ragged children playing in the dirt before the door vanished at the sight of him and reappeared to peep from the doorway once he had passed. These were the children whose attendance was poor, but he had so far failed to draw them into the school so that they lived half-wild in the moors. As he cycled on, he was conscious of their eyes and the eyes of their mother watching him suspiciously through the small kitchen window. Once, leaving the West Water, he rode along the road that skirted the foothills and then, pushing his bicycle, struck up a steep road that would take him over the shoulder of a hill which his inch-to-the-mile ordnance map told him was crowned by an Iron Age stronghold, and so down to the level country and the village. His route led him past a lonely farm, sheltering inadequately in a clump of pines, and on towards the earthworks he could see crowning the top of the hill. At the point where the gradient was about to change downwards he laid his bicycle on the grass by the wayside, crossed a five-bar gate and walked up the steep turf slope that led to the ancient fort.

If you climb the way he went over the short springy grass you reach a point on the ramparts of the fort where you can see the whole of Strathmore laid out before you, fertile, wooded, stretching out to where the North Sea imperceptibly slants towards the horizon. To the west and north are the hills that once formed some sort of frontier between the Lowlands and the Highlands, dark in spring, often white in winter, but in summer and especially in August purple with heather. When the fort was built the land below must have been bog, forest, scrub, full of game: deer, hare, pig in the woods, salmon and trout in the rivers, snipe, mallard, grey geese in the wet marshes and estuaries, grouse and partridge on the hillsides and, in the trees, blackcock and capercailzies. In the hills and forest, wolves. Up here on the plateau, behind the ramparts of loose stone, piled laboriously till they were twenty feet wide and high in proportion, they must have built their huts of skins or wattle, herded their sheep and cattle, hobbled their horses, gathered their late harvests from the field systems on the hillsides, watching perhaps for the flash of the sun on a spear or shield as the Romans pushed their reconnaissance up the coast with galleys, their sails clear to the naked eye, as their flankguard. This is the country that was ruled over by the strange hooded riders of the Pictish kingdom who have left scattered across it stone monuments with an intricacy of hippogriffs, serpents and strange geometrical designs or, on one splendid stone, a great leaping salmon. In winter the wind blows horizontally across the fort and there is little shelter even in the lee of the ramparts. In summer it is still cool but there is a curious depression seven or eight feet across — a storage pit perhaps— where you can lie and feel the heat of the sun and watch the clouds move overhead to dapple the strath with shadow. In August there is sometimes the noise of pooping guns as the shoot moves across the hill opposite or the grouse are driven on to the butts; but it is rare to meet anyone in the fort. Walking down you see — I see— the whole of my childhood and youth, from the village in its pinewood where I was born to the town by the sea with its great tidal estuary where I grew to adolescence, the spire of its parish clearly visible against the sea and with it the lighthouse that marks the mouth of the Esk. Within that fifteen miles by twenty rich in farms, with pastures, with its crops and fruit, and dotted with sheep, I grew up, was educated in a certain way, fantasticated through my adolescence, felt the first impulses of sex and then left for university, for the army, for those six years in which I grew up and changed. Each time I return I make my way to the fort and look out over the countryside in which, before these peripeties, I was formed, where so many things were seen, heard, felt to which I had no answers: mysteries spun by my parents, by visitors to the house, by the men and women I met in the streets of the village, to all of which I have still in some cases no solution and so can allow my fantasies to expand over that landscape in a game of recall and mystification that is at once a pain and a pleasure.

Turning round as he climbed the long slope to the fort to look seawards across the strath, he was surprised to see a little further on than his own a lady's bicycle lying by the roadside. He looked up towards the ramparts but could see no one. Perhaps it was the farmer's wife or daughter from the steading down the hill who had come up to gather the blaeberries he could see thick on the slopes; but there would have been little point in their pushing a bicycle up the hill since, going down, they would be hampered by a milk-pail of berries swinging on the handlebars and would have had to dismount rather than risk, so laden, a headlong ride. It was a bright clear day. Far out on the horizon he saw as a tiny white speck to the southeast the Bell Rock lighthouse some twenty miles out to sea. Farther south the coast of Fife formed a dark salient in the water. There was a little plume of smoke from the railway line that had brought him to Slateford. Once there was a booming noise from down the coast, repeated a few seconds later and followed by another report. The Territorials were at gunnery practice on their ranges by the sea. He imagined for a second that he saw the white plume where the shots plunged into the water of the sandbanks; but even as he looked he was aware that he was too distant to see the strike of the shells. To the south and east the coast was low but to the north he saw how it rose in high cliffs where the foothills of the Grampians came down to the sea. As he turned to resume his climb a brace of grouse scudded round the side of the hill. A few sheep wandered out of a clump of broom, eyed him for a moment and went on cropping the fine close grass. He passed the first ditch and its rampart. Time had loosened the stones and spread them out till they half-filled the ditch. After the second rampart he was in the fort itself. Patched with bracken and low blaeberry bushes it stretched in a wide oval plateau to the further wall beyond which the hill sloped steeply into the valley of some tributary of the West Water. There was no one to be seen. He walked over to the furthest edge and looked down to a lonely cottage on a patch of green turf, surrounded by sheep-folds. On the far side of the valley a shepherd was working his dogs. He could hear the distant thin whistle and an occasional shout and see the dogs flash through the bracken to round up the flock. The shadow of a cloud swept over the shepherd and his dog, slid down the hillside and in an instant had climbed up and over the fort. Suddenly the air felt cooler so that my father turned back fastening his jacket and began to make his way towards the entrance to the fort. About twenty yards inside the fort he became aware of a slight dip in the ground which, as he approached, he saw to be a depression some seven or eight feet across. Lying in it with her back against the side of the pit was a woman; she was reading. He stopped in indecision, not knowing whether to go on as if he had not seen her, to pass the time of day, or to withdraw and, making a circuit, reach the gateway in the ramparts by another route. Probably he made some slight noise — a twig of dry heath rustling against his boot — perhaps she, having felt the cloud sweep over, as he had, looked up in relief when the sun fell on her again. At all events look up she did, was startled to see a man standing on the edge of the sheltered spot she had found out of the wind, tugged with a reflex action at her skirt which showed an inch or two of white petticoat, then recovered herself and laughed: 'Ah,' she said, almost mockingly as it seemed to him, 'the new schoolmaster.' He took off his hat and said Yes he was the headmaster and then with a custom he presumably had picked up in France introduced himself: 'Scott.' She had risen to her feet and replied with a slight bow but he did not catch the name she gave. Holding out a hand with the utmost naturalness she invited him to help her up the slope to his side.

'I was reading,' she said, holding up her book, 'a fellow countryman of yours. David Hume. A wonderfully acute mind. Do you not agree? I like his view,' she turned a page to find the spot, 'that "the cause or causes of order in the universe have probably some remote analogy to human intelligence." '

Her English was easy and cultured but he seemed to detect something curious about her 'r's which were slightly burred — not in the French way but in a manner he had not heard before. His memories of Hume were limited to the reading of passages from the *Discourse of Human Knowledge* in his second year at University so that he could only mutter agreement. She went on to say that when Hume came back after his time in France he had almost forgotten how to write English. Yet he spoke so well. 'Do you know France?' she asked. Yes, he said, he had spent a year in Perpignan. 'Alors, vous aurez sans doute perfectionné votre français.' His answer was diffident but correct enough in its syntax and adequate in pronunciation.

They were walking together across the plateau. She interrogated him in a way that forced his pleasurable submission. She had not had the chance to speak to a Scotsman before; she wanted to know whether he, as one of them, did really feel different from, say, the English or the Irish or the Welsh. Frankly, she went on, of nationalism she was suspicious. Her interests were more international than national. For nationalism, he must admit, divided people. Internationalism united them. It was a theme he had heard expounded by some of the radicals among his fellow students but it surprised him that it should come from a young woman who was — to judge by her dress, appearance and manners — from a social category remote from the emotional socialism of student debating societies. They had passed through the ramparts and the landscape lay exposed before them.

'You see,' she said, 'there it is before us. The North Sea. And what do the Germans call it? The German Ocean. But the currents of the sea like the thoughts of great minds know no frontiers and no local patriotisms.'

Once free of the fort they walked on together for a little in silence; then she began to run downhill to the fence where she stopped and waited for him to join her. As he came down he wondered who she was, where she came from, how old she might be. Twenty-five, he thought, which was probably not far out. On the way down hill she took the corners with skill, braking momentarily and then letting her bicycle gather momentum, till at last they reached the level and to the whirr and tick of their freewheeling the impetus died out on the dusty road. It was four miles to the village, over the West Water and through fields where the corn was already being cut and stooked. A farmer watched the reaper at work and the men and women gathering the sheaves; he had his shotgun under his arm and waited for the rabbits to dash out when the last sheaves fell. As they cycled, my father noticed her rather large teeth and her grey eyes, the shadow of hair at the edge of her upper lip, the thickness of her dark hair. What surprised him, however, was her vigour and physical agility which some people, he knew, would have qualified as 'unladylike' but which he found challenging and exciting.

'There was a bird this summer,' she said, turning slightly in the saddle, 'It made a noise all night long so that I could hardly sleep. It reminded me of my childhood.' 'A corncrake,' he said, and wondered where that childhood had been spent. He had to repeat the name. She laughed and imitated the rasping call that all summer through had risen from the hay and young corn. 'Do you know the French for it? Caille, perhaps.' He thought that was 'quail' but he would look it up and let her know, he almost added, but hesitated to say so, being at sea in the matter of etiquette, not knowing how she might react.

Just past the first houses in the village she dismounted in front of a villa that stood back from the road on a knoll among a small plantation of pines. He dismounted too. She held out her hand. 'Au revoir, monsieur. Merci de la promenade et de la conversation.' As she pushed her bicycle into the drive of the villa he raised his hat. She turned and smiled.

I think they had met before. On the night he came to the village he was the last passenger to step on to the platform. In his hand was a scuffed Gladstone bag which he laid down for a moment to fasten his overcoat against the snell wind. Then he walked the length of the train — two carriages — to the guard's van to watch the porter extract his tin trunk and place it on a barrow. Together they moved towards the door where the stationmaster stood to collect a thin harvest of tickets from a couple of farmers back from some cattle mart and from a young woman with a brown fur muff and a brown veil over her face who moved off quickly into the darkness. A warm cloud of steam floated over from the engine to wreath itself around passengers, porter and stationmaster. When it had cleared there was a brief conversation. My father nodded and walked out into the station yard. Said the stationmaster to the porter: 'That'll be the new headmaster.'

I know the way he had come, changing at Glasgow, changing at Perth, waiting in the late afternoon at a wayside junction where the red-liveried London Midland and Scottish express dropped him to hang about for half an hour till the local train made the connection. Its engine was in the dark blue of the Caledonian Line; the seats were harder and dustier, the stops more frequent, the country stations dim islands of light in an obscure and unfamiliar landscape.

I know too the road he took from the station. It is easy to explain for the village — call it Slateford, one of the several names in its history — is laid out on a gridiron pattern: a long wide High Street with Church Street parallel to it and intersecting them, a couple of lanes with low cottages once the homes and workshops of the local weavers. Outside the station yard he had to turn left and then sharp right into Church Street, which runs due north so that, as he walked, he faced the range of hills that blocked the horizon. At the point where he encountered the first of the transverse lanes was the house he was looking for. On a corner site, solid, built of the local red sandstone. I can remember its owner when she was an old woman, dressed in black and hung about with jet beads, chasing away the children who played marbles against the wall of her front garden. Mrs Ramsay was her name, widow of an artist, whose shiny, dark brown canvases of Highland streams and Highland cattle she kept stacked along the walls of the studio with its north light that ran along the side of the house. How had my father found her? Possibly by some recommendation, some hint dropped by the secretary or chairman of the School Board the day he got the post: head-master of the village's three-teacher school.

The gate squeaked at his entrance so that he had little need to ring the bell. As he walked up the tiled path to the door he saw a woman's shadow fall across the drawn blind in the front room. His hand was still on the bell-knob when the same shadow filled the frosted glass of the front door. Mrs Ramsay opened and stood aside to let him pass into the lobby. She was a woman in her forties, buxom, handsome in her widow's clothes. 'Well, Mr Scott, it's a cold night. Come away in,' she said and indicated where he should set down his bag and hang his coat and hat. 'But the train was on time, I see.' Then she preceded him into the front room where there was warmth, a table laid for supper and an excess of furniture. 'Sit you down and draw in to the fire. Would you care for a drop of some-thing? Against the cold, I mean.' He made a gesture of modest refusal. 'Ah,' she said, 'a temperance man, are you? I like an occasional drop myself. For medical purposes, you under-stand.' He made a non-committal noise that confirmed her in the supposition that he had taken the pledge. 'I've made you high tea,' she went on. 'Nothing fancy. Guid Scots fare. My late husband — he was a painter you know and descended from Alan Ramsay,' her eyes went up to the opaque mountain landscape above the fireplace, 'he liked his meat. One of the lean kine though. In the end he fair wasted away. T.B.' She tapped her solid bosom.

The rest of her conversation that first evening as he ate the cold ham-roll, the home-made bannocks and scones was almost certainly a series of shrewd reconnaissances on her part to discover not only his preferences in terms of food and other creature comforts but his origins, his status (bachelor? engaged?) and his church membership. By the time he went upstairs to bed she might have put together this picture:

He came from Stirling with its castle rock, its garrison, its dubiously romantic history and its ring of coalmines and pithead bings. Mother — a widow and dressmaker in her spare time. Two brothers: one in Canada in the post office engineers; the other, clerk in a London shipping firm. Two sisters: one married to a fitter at the local colliery; the other unmarried and a shophand in a stationer's. Ex-student of Glasgow University. Member of the United Free Church. Last post — teacher in a junior school in Coatbridge under the shadow of the steel-works.

Some things she would have had to prise out of him. Some she learned only gradually, later. Others I am persuaded she was never able to get at. His age, for instance, which she had to guess and put at thirty, which was at least two years out. Or the fact that his abstemious refusal of a dram was due less to convinced puritanism — he had drunk wine in his time and in its place — than to the memory of his dead father, the jobbing gardener, drunk and melancholic, melancholic and drunk, sitting by the fire in a tenement flat and lamenting the money it took to put a boy through school and college when he might be earning his keep. He told her nothing either about his year in France, although he knew that sooner or later she must examine the labels on his trunk which spoke of his time in Perpignan. On the subject of his plans in life, in particular where marriage was concerned, he would be so blank as to persuade her that he was a confirmed bachelor, a perpetual lodger for whom it was a waste of time and money to provide the new schoolhouse that was rising on a feu just down the

24

road. Above all he was naturally and of necessity silent about those guilts he bore within him and which — when they surfaced in half-waking states, in dreams, but sometimes also in broad daylight — he experienced as a stigma setting him apart from all others, the source of obscure and ignorant terrors which led him to examine himself obsessively for outward and visible signs of a lapse from grace.

What one has to understand is that there was a lacuna, where his family was concerned, in my father's life — the year, to be precise, he spent in France. It is true that I occasionally came across vestiges of it among his books: a German grammar for French school-children from which in due course he taught me that language, two or three French novels with yellow paper covers and tattered spines bearing in his spidery hand the date and the name of a French provincial town. But what his experiences had been in that year he never discussed, never talked about them to his wife when we children were there (nor I suspect) when they were alone, never told us what he had eaten, how he had fared on a continental breakfast, reared as he was on a daily diet of porridge; what he did when he encountered cervelles au beurre noir or tripes à la mode de Caen (both of which his French landlady no doubt served up in her thrifty way); how he passed his evenings and his week-ends; where he went on New Year's Day or at Easter; how he coped with home-sickness. On a more trivial level there was no way of knowing how he had come to end up where he did — through what network of connections between the professor who ruled the lycée and the principal of this training college he had found the place and the opportunity. There was therefore this hiatus in his life, a gap of silence.

I remember the kind of bedroom in which he eventually unpacked his Gladstone bag and laid his nightgown on the bed. The wash-stand on which he arranged his lopsided shaving-brush, his half-used stick of shaving-soap and the pair of cut-throat razors in their leather case, had a ewer and basin decorated with dark red roses with a matching slop-pail underneath. He did not need to open the small door to one side of the stand to know that in it was a chamber-pot of similar pattern. The bed was high and narrow with at head and foot a framework of black metal tubing topped with brass knobs which with an automatic gesture he twisted tight on their screws. Above the bed some pious text. Lighten our darkness. Abide with me. Thou God seest me. On the opposite wall a brown photograph framed in dark wood. The face that looked out from it was pale, cold and curiously smooth like the face of a corpse. Mrs Ramsay as a girl? It reminded him of the sister a year younger than himself who had died and lain in her coffin in the front room with just such a face. The wardrobe tall, narrow, with a drawer beneath the mirror in which he laid a change of clothes, seemed to lean forward slightly as if it might fall full length across the rug and the dark linoleum beyond. The bed, when he got into it was hard with a dead weight of blankets. A cold room, for the narrow grate had never held a fire. Above the head of the bed and slightly to one side the gas-lamp's flame whispered in its incandescent mantle. Before he lay down to sleep he reached up to the chain that closed the valve and turned out the light. For a moment the mantle continued to glow red in the dark.

Next day he rose early. There was a hot-water can at his bedroom door, deposited with a discreet knock at half past seven. As he shaved he worked out a time-table and agenda for the day. Go to the manse. Get the keys. Look over the school. See the bank. Unpack the trunk which would meantime have been delivered by the station lorry. He ate his porridge, bacon and egg and hot mealy roll in solitude, avoiding Mrs Ramsay's attempts to begin any conversation beyond the ritual exchange about the weather which was indeed better, sunny with a hint of spring. Then he put on his coat and hat and walked over to the High Street and the corner where the haberdasher's windows modestly displayed female underwear, gloves, ribbons, handkerchiefs, reels of thread and hanks of wool. As he stood for a moment undecided which way to turn for the manse he saw a pony and trap come clip-clopping down the road from the north, across the Muir — the common land where the village streets ended with geometrical precision — and into the High Street. He saw, too, how as it passed a shopkeeper — the saddler, to be precise — made a slight inclination, the hint of a bow, as he hung the boots and horse-collars round the shop-door, and how, too, a couple of men removed their hats. As it drew nearer he could distinguish that at the reins was a woman with a feathered Highland bonnet and a suit trimmed with tartan. He thought it politic to remove his hat but did so with a certain inner reluctance, a lack of grace which the woman perhaps noticed and decided in her upper-class way to challenge.

'Good day,' she said in a high, light English-sounding voice that went curiously with her Highland gear, 'You must be Mr Scott, the new headmaster. I am Miss MacIllroy of the Burnfoot. My brother has told me about you. Welcome to Slateford. Good day to you.'

The wheels screeched on the loose metal of the road as she shook the reins and the pony started off. He put his hat back on his head. He was not used to such condescension nor such obligatory respect where he came from among the pitheads and the steelworks. Sister to Major MacIllroy of the Burnfoot, chairman of the School Board, master — in a certain sense — of his fate, he thought as he watched her drive off down the street.

One day Miss MacIllroy — much later — driving through the village with her pony and trap rebuked my mother because my brother, then seven, did not remove his cap promptly enough as she passed. I remember her as an old lady driving the same pony but by then one no longer required to show subservience to a decayed gentlewoman whose brother was dead and the fine timber of the Burnfoot estate cut down to pay off the death duties.

The Free Church manse was a four-square building facing south, parallel to the High Street, so that the front of the house looked over a sunny lawn to the flower garden. The side next to the street was darkly oppressive, dominated by a sombre monkey-puzzle tree (Araucaria imbricata) beneath which the grass had died for lack of light; a tall laurel hedge masked the tradesmen's entrance and a clump of holly bushes guarded the main gate. The polished bell-pull, set deep in the wall by the front door, brought quickly through the hall a teen-age girl with freckles and reddish hair. Her maid's uniform — black dress, white apron, and white frilled cap — sat oddly on her gauche and underdeveloped body. With a hint of suspicion she showed him into the drawing room where he stood uncertainly among the chintzes while she summoned the minister, a florid man who received his visitor with a wide gesture that was more welcoming than the tone of his voice or the expression of his quick darting eyes. Together they climbed the stairs to the study. As they passed her on the landing the maid flattened herself against the wall and looked nervously down at her feet. In the study: a large desk, a lectern, a wall of books. Prominent on the desk a Concordance to the Old and New Testaments, the pool in which the minister fished for texts and inspiration for his sermons. On the shelves: volumes of pietistics and theology. A Latin, a Greek and a Hebrew dictionary. Lives of missionaries and accounts of their labours in darkest Africa or the mysterious East. Biographies of Scottish divines. A history of the Church in Scotland. A history of the Disruption, the great schism in the Scottish Church in 1843. Stale pipe-smoke clung to the black horse-hair on which the minister indicated his visitor should sit. He himself sat in a deep leather sofa by the window. There was a silence as each waited for a gambit.

The minister began:

'Well, you've brought the end of winter at any rate, Mr Scott. *Diffugere nives* — as the poet says.' The Latin tag served to establish his academic standing. 'You're more than welcome. We have been waiting for you. You are Free Church, are you not? So I seem to recall from your interview in which, if I may say so, you acquitted yourself very well. Very well indeed. Mind you the parish minister wasn't too well pleased. He'd have preferred someone who would sit under him of a Sunday and be at his beck and call.' He gave a slight smile. 'You mustn't misunderstand me. We're on excellent terms and exchange pulpits once a year. It makes a change for our respective flocks. In any case the Disruption has been behind us for a good many years and there's no point in reviving old scores.' He paused for a second. 'Now we have a kirk session next week. I fully expect that they will want you to join them as an elder. No objection, I take it? Most important I find it that you set an example to the young. I always say that just as the fear of God is the beginning of wisdom so religious instruction in school is the very bedrock of education. You answered well on that in the interview. It got you my vote, I may say. I like myself to drop into the school a couple of times a year — nothing formal, of course — just to test the bairns on their knowledge of scripture and catechism. Now about your sitting. There's a pew vacant. The occupant was taken from us last winter. Very sad. A retired shepherd. The Lord giveth, the Lord taketh away. You're a bachelor, I seem to remember, but you'll be going to settle down now among us and set up a family no doubt. The blessing of a good wife is inestimable. More precious than rubies as the Bible puts it. Children too — a great comfort, a great comfort. In this respect I have been greatly blessed. Let us offer up a prayer for your time here among us.'

The headmaster bowed his head and listened as the voice changed to a different key and a different intonation and called down on our new headmaster the guidance of the Most High and the wisdom which only Thou, Lord, canst impart. For the sake of Jesus Christ, our Lord, Amen. And as he listened he thought of what Mrs Ramsay had told him the evening before in their exchange of confidences of the minister's wife, how well connected she was and how she had brought the Reverend James Murdoch, whose father was not much more than a crofter up one of the glens, a pretty penny in marriage as well as six children, all sons.

There was a pause and another effortless change of tone.

'Now about the keys to the school. You'll get them from Willie Hamilton just up the High Street — opposite the smithy. A good man, Willie. He's your school caretaker and my beadle. Sees to the cleaning. Lights the boiler for the school kitchen. Keeps the place tidy. A handyman, too. Mrs Murdoch swears by him. And if you have a rod Willie's your man to show you where to take a fish or two when the salmon are running. One thing — don't be too free with the gratuities. He'll only drink it. But he's a dab hand with the scissors. Does my hair and the boys' as well.' The minister ran his hand over his thin hair. 'Well then, Mr Scott, I must be getting on with my sermon. I wrestle with it like Jacob with the angel. But it's a sair fecht sometimes.'

'Yes,' said the other. '*Orare est laborare*'. In terms of Latinity the scores were now even.

Having imagined this man, this John Scott, headmaster of the three-teacher school in the village of Slateford, how can I account for the following paradox: that on the one hand he was in terms of religious belief tepid to the point of agnosticism and that, on the other, he found it important to proclaim his adherence to the Free Church, to one form of Presbyterianism rather than another — the other being the Established Church, incarnate as it were, in the parish church building (built 1819, 650 seatings but seldom more than a quarter full) which dominated the village from its site on the Muir. His agnosticism I would explain by his time in France, that year spent teaching in the lycée in Perpignan and to his exposure to the radical scepticism of his French colleagues, Dreyfusards and republicans, who defended the lay order of the Third Republic against political and religious reaction. His membership of the United Free Church derived from his knowledge that as headmaster membership of one or other church would be expected of him, that indeed it was an unspoken condition of his appointment along with the acknowledgement of the importance of religious instruction in the curriculum, his ready acceptance of which had won the vote of the Reverend James Murdoch. But in choosing his ecclesiastical allegiance, which was determined by such considerations, there also came into play the inertia of family habit and tradition and something slightly more principled, something with a hint of politics, or — to put it less strongly — of social choice behind it.

In social terms had he joined the parish church and gone indeed to 'sit under' its minister, the Reverend Tom Arnott, he would have found himself as an elder walking up the aisle, tendering the collection bag at the end of its long polished wooden pole to the big farmers of the parish and sharing the communion cup with the agent of the local branch of the British Linen Bank, with the solicitor from the nearby market town and the owner of the Central Hotel in Church, the howff where these same farmers forgathered for a dram or two or more after the sheep marts and cattle marts and the feeing markets where they hired their ploughmen and shepherds. By adhering to the Free Church he might be said to have placed himself in class terms, and would find himself elected elder by a kirk session composed of the village tailor, the village butcher, a couple of small farmers and the owner of the grocery store. So it would come about that he would stand beside the collection plate at the church door on Sundays in his frock coat and high stiff collar and greet the liberal elements of village society reinforced by a number of incomers: a retired teacher or two, a pensioned minister, a number of ladies, widowed or single, of independent means and evangelical opinions and — in summer — visiting professional men from Edinburgh, Glasgow or Dundee holidaying in the village with their families. But not the fathers and mothers of most of the children who would pass through his hands. They were too dependent on the parish and its patronage in the way of jobs for the girls as maids in the big houses round about, for the boys as apprentices and messenger-boys, for their mothers as washerwomen and cleaners. So they sat dutifully among their betters and endured the dry fare of the Reverend Tom Arnott's sermons. From both congregations two notable figures were missing: the Major and his sister. They were Episcopalians as became their rank and upbringing in England — 'Piskeys' who worshipped, when they worshipped, in the market town which had an Episcopalian church and a bishop: a fact that brought them perilously close to Popery.

Willie Hamilton's cottage had been a weaver's home when there were still linen-weavers in Slateford: two rooms — a but and a ben, they called them — separated by a corridor that ran from front to back door and, affixed to the gable-end, the workshop which had once housed the loom. It gave the whole a curiously lopsided air and qualified it for its description as 'a house and a half'. Willie had ginger hair and a slight cast in one eye. A man in his fifties he bore the shabby marks of negligent bachelordom. He bade his visitor to go 'ben the house' and invited him to share a cup of tea from the pot that simmered on the hob. He was, he explained, a single man — like yourself, they tell me — who had almost got married once but then had gone off to enlist and to the wars. He had been on Majuba Hill with the Scottish Fusiliers. That was a terrible day. They Boers, they could shoot you through the eye at a couple of hundred yards. Then he had been in India — Bangalore, the Frontier, Delhi for guard duty on the Viceroy's residence. Aye, it was a great time and a great chance to see a bit of the world. After a while he hadna missed a wife. There are always women. But what he missed now was lying on his charpoi — that's a kind of string bed — and being shaved as he slept by the Indian barber. Aye, while he slept. You'd hardly credit it but it was true. The headmaster sipped his thick tarry tea and decided he would hear plenty soldier's tales in future and with a sudden gesture of authority and dismissal rose and asked for the keys. 'Oh aye, the keys. Here they are, Mr Scott. Would you have me come up to the school and show you which is which?' The offer was refused. 'And if you want anything — a

32

haircut, a rod or a cast of flies, just ask me.' Although I imagine that what he actually said was: 'Just speir at me.'

The headmaster nodded non-committally and was off up the road.

The school is a squat, solid building in the shape of a T with a short stem and a long stroke. It lies at the most northerly point of the village. On the other side of the road, to the north, is the Muir and the parish church, a plantation concealing the rubbish dump, an old curling pond — in the spring it was full of copulating frogs and their spawn — and further away, at the other end of the Muir, a pine copse where the tinkers used to set up their round-roofed tents and work at their business of mending broken china, patching saucepans, and fashioning pot-scrubbers out of dry heather. When I knew the school the stem of the T housed the infants. We stood in a circle on the floor round the infant mistress's chair and chanted c-a-t CAT or two times one are two, two times two are four or played singing games — The farmer wants a wife, The wife wants a child Hey ho my daddy oh The wife wants a child — or else passed bags of beans to one another in a mild gymnastic exercise. The stroke of the T was divided into two classrooms by a sliding partition, glass halfway down. In one the juniors sat at desks ranged one above the other. Their slates squeaked as they added, divided, multiplied and subtracted. They too chanted tables: four gills one pint two pints one quart four quarts one gallon eight gallons one bushel. Each week there was a test followed by a ceremonial rearrangement of seats as pupils were promoted up to the back of the class or brought down to join the dunces in the front under the eye of the young woman teacher and so easily accessible for supervision or the occasional clout on the head for fidgeting or inattention. But the real fear was to be sent through the partition to where the headmaster ruled. There before the expectant senior school the victim had to announce that he — it was usually a boy — had come for punishment. Then the leather tawse came out of the headmaster's desk, split at the end, black and snake-like. Afterwards the victim would come back with swollen hands and a begrutten face into a hush in which every child held its breath and the whole room bent over their slates. Occasionally a big boy from the seniors was dragged out of the classroom to be threshed in the seclusion of the staffroom. Then the whole school was still, listening, until the woman teacher said sharply: 'Get on with your work now.' These were terrible and strangely exciting, disturbing moments. My father was the headmaster.

When the new headmaster found the right key and opened the door that led from the girls' playground the corridors were dark and smelt of polish and disinfectant, for it was Easter holiday time and the school would be closed for a week. The tiles as he entered rang under his feet. In the staffroom on his left as he came in at the door there was a cupboard with modelling clay on the shelves wrapped, he noted with satisfaction, in damp cloths, and a trunk full of raffia. He put in his hand and drew out a skein of purple fibre. The smell clung to his fingers as he explored further. An inner door led, as he suspected, to the toilet. There were a couple of chairs, a table and a coat rack. It would, he felt, probably be the territory of the two women teachers: Miss Troup and Miss Kerr. In the infant classroom he pushed the balls on the abacus in its high frame and listened to how they clicked. The seats of the desks were folded back. There was a large fireplace with a high guard round the hearth topped by a brass rail. He could guess how in wet or snowy weather the children from the outlying farms and cottarhouses would hang their coats and jackets on the rail; as they dried they would give off an unforgettable smell of farm life, of dung, corn, oatmeal, urine and poverty.

In the juniors a hymn had been written on the long blackboard in tonic solfa: All things bright and beautiful. Not a bad tune if one had to sing hymns. The words and the music carefully written. By Miss Troup. He wondered what she looked like. How they would work together. Then he slid back the partition and entered his own room.

In the desk there was a half-full box of white chalk and a duster for the blackboard alongside the attendance registers for each class. He looked at the names: David Torrie, Davina Jackson, Dorothy Leighton, Rosemary Watson, Frank Low. Unremarkable names. There were a couple of bad attendance records. He would have to look into the reasons for them. In the bookcase and cupboard the exercise books were piled tidily enough. Compositions in laborious slanting writing with the up-strokes very fine and the down-strokes firm and thick. Problems of the usual kind: If it takes two men 6 days to dig a trench 50 feet long, how long will they take to dig a trench of the same depth 270 feet long? He was dubious about the usefulness of such calculations to children who in a couple of years would be working at the tail of the plough or milking cows or — like the girl at the manse — in service as housemaids. Although there were others who would find their way with luck to a secondary school and so escape from the village and a life on the land, emigrating perhaps to Canada, the States or New Zealand. Not many books on the shelves and those there were old-fashioned. His predecessor, as he drew towards retirement had been content to stick in the old ways and the old methods. On the high window ledge a stuffed fox gave off a cloud of fine dust when he patted its fur. It was flanked by an adder and a toad in tall jars, preserved in spirits. Age had given them a curious yellow hue that could hardly be natural. On the other window a stuffed owl squinted down on the classroom with its one remaining eye. He would get rid of them all. Buy a decent globe for geography. A balance in a glass case for chemistry. Coloured chalks. Paint and paint brushes. Some decent books: Stevenson. Scott. Hume Brown's History of Scotland. A dictionary. Basic salts for experiments in chemistry. Beneath the windows in a long cupboard were maps — tattered maps of the British Isles and the world in Mercator's projection, frayed at the edges and cracked from careless rolling. He would order new maps. Get the support of the Inspector to push his demands through the School Board. At the very back a diagram of the human body and its organs. It was impossible to determine the sex for the secondary sexual characteristics were fudged and the reproductive organs sketchily indicated. He looked at it with a mixture of interest and revulsion for he had a fear of blood and of entrails. He must tell Mrs Ramsay that he did not eat liver or kidney or lights. Walking out of the building he turned down past the workshop which smelt strongly and, as he felt, healthily of woodshavings and timber. The benches were orderly and the tools well cared for, the planes and chisels slightly oiled; he had seen schools where things were less well kept. Perhaps his predecessor had been keen on carpentry. Beyond the workshop was a low-roofed shelter flanked by the lavatories. In the boys' urinal green mould flourished on the walls but the place smelt clean. Willie Hamilton apparently did his job. At the back of the shelter where roof and whitewashed wall joined there were the remains of the nests built by last year's swallows and house-martins. In a couple of months they would be back, swooping in under the eaves with a sure tilt of the wings and a flash of white breast.

As he walked away from the school and turned down the High Street towards the bank he was aware of eyes watching him from behind windows and through shop doors. The new dominie, someone commented in the post office. Yes, the name is Scott, the saddler told a customer as he bundled up a pair of re-soled boots. No — he's not married or engaged, said Mrs Ramsay in the butcher's as she paid for the chop that would be his dinner. The thought of these eyes and of the comments that must accompany their glances made him feel curiously exposed and conscious of his own movements — the way he placed his feet, the way he moved his arms — so that it was with a feeling of relief that he walked into the bank. There was another customer, a young woman, at the wide desk that rose in a slope of dark polished wood to a peak guarded by a fine brass trellis. Behind it a clerk worked at the great ledgers with their leather bindings and blue and pink marbled edges; but he merely looked up to say the agent was busy and went on with his careful entries. Behind the counter an open door showed a small room with barred windows. Hidden from sight by the door was no doubt the safe and the strong boxes for deeds, wills and jewellery, for there was sound of shutting and locking before the agent emerged carrying a document and came round through the little wicket-gate at the end of the counter to discuss it with the young woman. The teacher stood to one side demonstrating inattention but looking at her whenever he felt he could do so without being seen. She was fairly tall with a strong, handsome face, the nose somewhat prominent, the mouth full and mobile with a shadow of hair at the corners of the upper lip. Her complexion was slightly sallow but the skin was clear and healthy. Her dark hair was looped over her ears. The long brown dress with its tight fur-trimmed jacket had what he recognized as a stylish cut. It was not for nothing that he had studied fashion pictures his mother bought, developing an eye for such matters together with a sensuous pleasure in the texture of a sample of cloth, a remainder of silk or crêpe-de-chine (which he would steal and keep to relish its smoothness) together with a consuming, frightening interest in what might lie beneath the outward clothing of the women, thin-waisted, large-busted, somehow unreal, that inhabited the pages of fashion journals. As it was he had had only one experience which, when it surfaced in his memory, he dismissed as too exceptional, too improbable, to serve as a guide to what the lady standing there exploring a crack in the floor with the tip of her umbrella, might wear beneath her suit, or what sort of body went with the face that now opened into a smile as she thanked the agent, glanced at the clerk, allowed her eyes to pass over his face and walked past to the door. The agent was there before her, urgently courteous. As he bowed her out he used her name but the teacher did not catch it. When she was gone the agent turned and asked: 'And what can I do for Mr . . . ? 'Scott,' said the other. 'Ah, yes — Mr Scott,' said the agent. 'Good of you to look in.' His business was soon over. His salary of £25 a month would be paid directly into his account. He had a certain amount of savings which he would transfer from his previous bank to a deposit account. No, he had so far no standing charges to meet. An insurance? the agent suggested. He would think it over. As he walked away his mind still ran on the young woman whom he thought perhaps he might have seen before — as she offered her ticket to the stationmaster with a slim gloved hand and, adjusting her veil over her face, walked out of the station into the dark.

Why, I must ask myself, do I introduce her into my fantasies? For there can be no doubt that it is H. who died eight years ago succumbing to cancer — so I learned — which no doubt she fought as stubbornly as she fought other obstacles in life. It was not for nothing, she told me with a grin, that her family nickname had been 'Böckchen', the little goat. I could have mentioned her rather large teeth and her grey eyes in one of which there was a tiny white scar where something had cut the eyeball — what, why and where she would not reveal out of, I suspect, a love of mystery and the need to have secrets. I can remember the feel of her thick rather coarse hair and how she like to feel my hands run through it to the nape of her neck, how her breathing quickened and grew stronger and she turned to kiss me. Her body was long and slim for she was a good swimmer, was swift and daring on skis, had flown planes. Like her face the skin of her body was slightly dark, the nipples brownish, her breasts full. Her movements as she opened her body to my exploration expressed a sensuality which she both succumbed to and resented. So that when our lovemaking was over she withdrew into a kind of privacy;

when she had dressed and combed her hair her behaviour was almost formal as if she wished to put a distance between herself and what had taken place a few minutes before. Her voice was low with a slightly defective 'r' which sounded strange among her well-coached, cultured, upper-class vowels. What she said reflected the tough intelligence of her mind, her knowledge, her humour. Sometimes she would reflect with mocking irony on the strangeness of chance that had brought us together and the curious fact that, stemming from such different cultures, we still had so much in common: books read, pictures seen, music heard, languages understood. Sometimes I felt that this too disturbed her; sometimes she accepted it as merely another less cruel twist of the cards than that which had landed her, a refugee, in a country where she had slowly learned to adopt other modes of behaviour, different standards, from those of a comfortable Jewish family in Munich with their seats at the Opera, their holidays in Tuscany and the false security that came from conversion and assimilation. We parted — as lovers at least — in a Fleet Street coffee-house; I wept silently, uncontrollably.

After his dinner of shepherd's pie and rice pudding he went out again. A hundred yards down the road from Mrs Ramsay's — he had passed the site without being aware of it in the dark of the previous evening — he paused to watch the men at work on the schoolhouse: the house where he would be expected to live and settle down to marriage and the raising of a family. The stonework was still low — only a couple of courses. The soil round the building site was trampled and hard. Beyond that was unbroken field stretching twenty yards or so to a high sandstone wall. It would take months of work to dig up the grass and to break the soil where the boots of the builders and the wheels of the carts had compacted it. He could see clearly the plan of the building: two front rooms, a kitchen and a scullery, a small room at the side of the house — a bedroom perhaps. How would he live in it? With whom? The future was vague and obscure. He felt at once excited and afraid.

He walked on past the Free Church, which was in the next feu. A green-painted notice-board announced that the Rev James Murdoch, MA, BD, was minister; that there were services at 11 and 6 on Sundays, Sunday School at 12.30, Communion Service once a month, Women's Guild on Thursdays. He reflected that he would inevitably be drawn to the activities of the church, that he would have for years perhaps to listen to the Rev James Murdoch's harangues to the Almighty, listen to newly graduated divines trying their sermons on a country congregation and take his turn by the collection plate. At least he could say without deceit that he was no singer and could therefore not be impressed into the choir. He shrugged his religious duties off internally, as it were, and continued past the station to the village hall, the gift of a great landed proprietor in memory of a son killed at that battle on Majuba Hill in the high veldt where Willie Hamilton had heard the bullets of the Boer marksmen go past like angry bees. He sat down in the high Gothic library with its stained-glass windows blue and red and white with the blazonry of the noble lord whose real wealth came through marriage into a family of cotton-thread manufacturers in Paisley, the wife a pale delicate creature always in mourning for her only son and refusing to take comfort from the parallel urged upon her by her husband that the Prince Imperial, nephew of the Emperor Louis Napoleon, had died at the same age, struck down by an assegai in the Zulu wars. A tablet on the wall between the two main windows was dedicated to the memory of Second Lieutenant the Honourable Alasdair Keir-Ramsay, 1st Battalion, the Scottish Fusiliers, who lost his life in the service of his Queen, etc. at the age of eighteen. Beneath the plaque a framed brown cutting from *The Times* briefly recorded the circumstances. The headmaster sat down at one of the sombre tables and looked at the shelves filled with bound back numbers of the *Illustrated London News, Punch,* the *Scotsman* and the

Glasgow Herald, Church magazines and improving books. Taking a gazetteer from the shelves he might have read this about the village and its parish:

SLATEFORD, a parish partly in Kincardineshire but chiefly in Forfarshire. It contains a post-office village of that name. Its length is 12¾ miles and its greatest breadth is 4½ miles. Its southern part is a sort of peninsula, the East and West Waters flowing along its limits and forming a confluence under the name of the North Esk at its extremity. In the western and northern part the parish is hilly; but in the southern section it is more open and well-sheltered by plantation. The greater part of the parish being bleak and unsheltered, the air is generally strong and piercing but is not insalubrious. The southern part of the parish belongs all to Lord Panmure. Three of those monuments of antiquity called Druidical temples are in the parish; two within a few yards of each other at Culindir and one at Dalbog. They consist of tall upright stones enclosing elliptical spaces, the largest being 45 feet long by 36 feet. The castle at Slateford is a magnificent ruin. It consists of two stately towers connected by an extensive wall. The proprietors of this castle, the Lindsays, surpassed in power any family in the county. The village of Slateford began to undergo great improvement in 1839 and is now a beautiful assemblage of neat stone houses with flower plots in front of them, surrounded by pleasant scenery and much frequented by summer lodgers. There are in the parish a woollen mill and about 50 linen looms. The parish church was built in 1818 and contains 650 sittings. There is a Free Church, attendance 460.

The gazetteer was out of date even then. There was no more flax growing on the farms around the village so the linen looms were gone although the wool mill remained — as it did throughout my own childhood. It stood on the other side of the East Water. A long slanting dam that reached almost from one bank to the other diverted some of the water from the river into a mile-long lade to drive the great wheel that worked the tweed looms. Unlike the water in the river bed, which passed through a sequence of rapids, that of the lade ran smoothly. Long green water-weeds undulated in the bottom. A few small trout or maybe large minnows lurked in their shadow. The banks were thick with umbelliferae that gave off a strong aromatic scent when their stalks were crushed or broken. We sucked the juice and called the plant myrrh. At the sluice set half-way along the lade to control the volume of water when the river was in spate there was a constant seepage, a damp trickle into a watercourse on the banks of which the globe-flowers raised their gleaming yellow balls. Today the lade is dry; the slanting dam that drew off the water has crumbled in the floods; the machinery of the sluice is rusted solid. The mill has gone. But in the village itself little has changed. Except for the American cars and the accents of the children who cycle past. They belong — children and cars — to the American servicemen who operate the great listening-post in the flat land of the strath beyond the river. On an old aerodrome from the First World War, now much enlarged, electronic dishes cock their ears to the sky and radar detectors whirl incessantly. Aerials — delicate antennae — point eastward towards the rocket bases in the Soviet Union. No doubt in some deep operations bunker in Russia these installations are ringed as first strike targets for the rockets that lie waiting snugly in their silos. The ring cannot fail to encircle the whole village as well.

When he got back his tin trunk had arrived. Mrs Ramsay had given the carter a few coppers; these he repaid at once. But he refused her offer to help him upstairs with the trunk, preferring to raise it slowly step by step and so across the landing to his bedroom, although he knew that by now she must have examined and speculated upon every label on it. The clothes he put in the wardrobe: his morning-coat for church-going and for funerals, his winter coat, his best suit — the one he had worn for the interview with the School Board — his old suit for gardening and (it might be) for fishing. In the drawer beneath went his underwear, socks and shirts, the stiff collars he must wear for special occasions — like the visit of His Majesty's Inspector of Schools — coiled in their leather box. Once the clothes were out of the way he could proceed to lay out his books. Mrs Ramsay had provided a small bookcase into which there went his Greek New Testament, the Bible his mother had given him for his sixteenth birthday, some Latin textbooks from University — Tacitus, Caesar's *De Bello Gallico*, Horace's *Odes Book IV*, the *Aeneid* — then the volumes he had collected in France — *Les Fables* de La Fontaine, Flaubert's *Madame Bovary, Moeurs de Province* (with as an appendix the proceedings against the author before the Paris Criminal Court for offences against religion and public morality, the defence and the judgement), Voltaire's *Candide, Lettres de Mon Moulin* by Daudet, Racine and Corneille, a volume of de Maupassant's short stories — lastly the edition of Scott's Waverley Novels which he was buying one a month, the copy of *David Copperfield* he had won as a school prize, a *Golden Treasury of English Poetry* and a collection of school textbooks which were, so to speak, the tools of his trade. Last of all came his editions of Gibbon's *Decline and Fall of the Roman Empire* and Buckle's *History of Civilisation* in which Mrs Ramsay, if her curiosity took her so far, might find the following passages marked with a double line of approbation in the margin:

I challenge anyone to contradict my assertion, when I say that nearly all over Scotland the finger of scorn is pointed at every man who, in the exercise of his sacred and inalienable right of free judgement, refuses to acquiesce in those religious notions and to practice those religious customs which time indeed has consecrated but many of which are repulsive to the eye of reason.

And again, further on:

> I do deliberately affirm that in no civilised country is toleration so little understood and that in none of them is the spirit of bigotry and of persecution so extensively diffused.

Mrs Ramsay would no doubt have found herself questioning the suitability of the new headmaster for his post and have considered his acceptance of the status of elder in the Free Kirk an act of total cynicism; but another observer, like myself, would be more inclined to say — looking at the narrow and fairly conventional composition of the library — that here was someone who was on the brink of intellectual explorations but who perhaps lacked the impetus to take him further.

Freud describes as 'family romances' the manifold ramifications of the imaginative activity which children apply to the sex life of their parents — an activity which he associates closely with the business of writing, success in which he believes requires 'the courage to let the unconscious speak'. There is a sense in which this is a 'family romance'. Why else should my imagination play round the figure of my father who was indeed a village schoolmaster but yet not the man I see walking through the streets of Slateford with his bowler hat and Gladstone bag? A figure who is and is not my father just as 'I' am I and not I. For there is an 'I' who tells the story, the hypostasis of my memories and fantasies, the assemblage of hypotheses and possibilities into which I spill thoughts and feelings that spring from some source suddenly accessible to me, producing what is not truth yet should have a feel of being some contingent truth about it. Meanwhile there is the I who sits today in 1984 and types these words on to the page while that other 'I' becomes the carrier (as it were), the conductor of a strange obsessive process which is at once pleasurable and questionable. For why, on the face of it, should it matter or be of interest to anyone except myself that I should by such indirections attempt to make from half-understood hints, snatches of conversation and images from childhood a picture of the social, economic and political ambiance that conditioned the life of John Scott, who is — I repeat not my father — but someone he might have been with whom I share some characteristics: so much that I can allow him to appropriate the memory of H. So a 'family romance' in which the analyst might find rich matters to discuss.

The 'father' who is not my father and whose son is not I but the voice through which I speak, came to Slateford and settled in 1908 or 1909 — the date is not important. It would be tedious to go over the steps by which he worked himself into his new post; how he inevitably brushed with Miss Kerr, the infant teacher, whose methods were those of a dame school and who had, in fact, begun teaching with a little class in her own kitchen; how he worked well with Miss Troup, the teacher of the juniors, who had been a pupil-teacher in Edinburgh's Canongate and had learned there to stand her ground against uproar, rebellion and anarchic lack of discipline in the great classes of ragged combative children of the slums; how he avoided contact with her out of school, although she went to the same church and indeed sang in the choir, not because he did not like her but out of awkwardness — an inability to know how to behave towards her in any situation other than a professional one. Yet there were times when he admitted to himself that there was a certain expectancy in the way he watched for her to come up the steps to the church door and drop a sixpence in the collection plate, dark-haired and slightly flushed.

In that first summer term he learned much about the village

and the countryside around it. How the country children set out from home to walk their two, three or even four miles to school wearing their hobnailed boots and how once out of sight of home they took off their boots, hid them in a hedge and ran on kicking up the dry dust with their hard feet. How in June there was a horse fair with sideshows and booths at Trinity which the boys in particular truanted to attend, coming to school next day with some trifle from the shooting booths stuck in their lapels to receive the punishment he felt required to deal out to them. Yet his attitude to corporal punishment — to the use of the tawse — was ambivalent. The educational system in which he had grown up and of which he was now a part was firmly based on the concept that to spare the rod was to spoil the child. It was, he recalled, a senior lecturer at training college with silvery hair and a great reputation for Christian works who taught that new teachers must establish their authority speedily by belting a couple of pupils — it did not greatly matter who they were or for what reason they were punished. But the class would know that the teacher meant business. He was reminded of that Old Testament prophet whom the boys taunted about his grey beard and how the Lord sent a bear to eat them up. But he knew no way yet of breaking out of the trap; for what the teacher threatened the pupils expected and would have held him in contempt (so he argued) had he abjured the tawse.

In due course the Reverend James Murdoch came and tested the children on their knowledge of the Gospels and the catechism, enquiring of them 'What is man's effectual calling?' and getting the chanted response: 'Man's effectual calling is to glorify God'. Though what effectual calling meant they would have been hard put to it to explain. But the minister declared himself satisfied. He was naturally followed by the Reverend Tom Arnott, the parish minister, who was somewhat fiercer and interrogated the children sharply; What was the name of David's father? How old was Samuel when he entered the temple? How many books are there in the Old Testament? What comes after the Book of Habbakuk? What was the name of Ruth's mother? Grudgingly he had to admit that they seemed to have a good knowledge of Scripture but felt that when he came next he would wish to hear them recite some extended passage like: Tell it not in Gath, publish it not in the streets of Askalon and so on. 'Little by little, Mr Scott,' he said, 'line upon line.' The Inspector of Schools came too in the early summer. Together they discussed methods, textbooks and the aims of education. 'Education is the basis of Scotland's greatness, Mr Scott. There's many a lad — many a ploughman's son and daughter too, for that matter — that's gone on from a school like yours to better things,' said the Inspector over Mrs Ramsay's chicken broth with which she had been at great pains because of the importance of the guest. 'Think of all these lads in Australia, in Canada and in India even who might never have been able to take their chance if people like you — and your colleagues — had not laid a sound basis in the three R's and given them a real foundation on which to build. But of course you need discipline to go with it. Mind you I don't think, like some folk I could mention — people like old Carson at your training college — who used to go on as if knowledge could be belted in with a length of leather. But when I came into school this morning and saw the bairns sitting there with their arms folded and then saw them get up and say 'Good morning sir' loud and clear, I said to myself, this is a school where there is discipline, this is a school where they can learn. To be quite honest and between you and me and the gatepost your predecessor who was a decent old stick but very narrow, very narrow, had let things run down a bit. No real method, I believe myself in regular tests. Children must learn to strive. Excelsior, I say. And to him that overcometh a crown of life is given.' There was a pause. 'Remarkable broth your landlady makes. You're well found here, Mr Scott. But you'll not be able to live in digs for ever — there's that fine schoolhouse they're building up the road. There's nothing for it but marriage. No doubt you'll be thinking it over — looking about you — unless there's someone half-spoken already. No? Then take my advice, don't rush it.

Marriage is for a long time. So tak' tent, as they say in good broad Scots.'

'Tak' tent' he did — indeed took so much care that his courtship, (if it could be called that) of May Mitchell went slowly. On the other hand it was with a strange, unaccustomed recklessness that he allowed his thoughts to play round that other woman with her curiously precise, bookish English and her agile body. How he wondered, could he legitimately get in touch with her — renew the conversation begun on the hill-top fort.

When he got home after their meeting he looked up 'corn-crake' in his French dictionary; there was no such entry. He felt an inordinate sense of disappointment, the fading of a fantasy in which he wrote a formal letter in well-turned French, scrupulously scanned for errors, and written in his finest copper-plate hand with thin up-strokes and full down-strokes. On the capital letters he would allow himself a slight flourish — as on the opening words: Mademoiselle — or Madame? — Je me permets. But when he was fantasizing over the super-scription of his letter he became soberly aware that he did not know her name or whether she was married or unmarried; the name he had not heard and had felt too shy to ask her to repeat it. In either case it would hardly do for him to write to her on the strength of a chance meeting, a half-hour bicycle ride and a conversation interrupted by the need to watch out for potholes or by the labour of pushing their bicycles up the switchback rises of the road. I imagine it must have taken a little time and thought before he decided to sound out Mrs Ramsay, his caution being due to his observation that she was remarkably quick to seize on a clue — the postmark on a letter, a chance remark in conversation, a label on his trunk — to develop a theory which she would explore gradually over a period of days or weeks until she had to her own satisfaction found a rationale for the phenomenon and was, she felt, in a position to state it as a matter of undisputed fact to her friends at the Women's Guild as they sat and knitted socks or sewed shirts for missionaries in distant fields of endeavour. There was a danger, therefore, that even by posing a question about the villa at the edge of the village and its occupants he would set her off on a train of romantic speculation. Nevertheless it was a risk he was seriously thinking of taking when one morning in September, a Saturday, he was sitting at his breakfast reading the *Glasgow Herald* with some distaste, for it was fulminating against Liberals, when there was a noise of horse's hooves coming up Church Street from the stables by the station — a noise that brought Mrs Ramsay through, on the pretext of clearing the table, so that she might see, drawing back the heavy red plush curtains slightly, who the rider might be. My father turned in his chair too to look. It was the lady of the railway station, of the bank, of the fort, of the bicycle ride. She rode side-saddle, managing her horse easily when it pranced skittishly at a shadow or blown leaf. Her habit was black with a white stock at the neck and a veil over her face beneath the tall riding hat. As she passed she gathered the horse for a second, leaning forward to pat its neck, then rode off towards the Muir where no doubt she would let it break into a canter or gallop up to the woods that sheltered the village from the north winds. Her passing gave him a cue to ask who she was and to add disingenuously that he hadn't seen her in church.

'Neither your church nor mine,' said Mrs Ramsay, whose allegiance was to the parish church. 'She's been here a six-month and hasn't been inside a church yet. Maybe she's a Piskey like the folk at the Burn. But I know the Major's cook and she has it from the coachman that when the laird and his sister drive over to chapel he's never seen her there either. Maybe she's an R.C. She keeps herself to herself alone in that big house with a kind of housekeeper that never goes out. I've heard tell that there's a couple of children has arrived lately — in their teens. So they can't be hers. Some folk say she's a foreigner and can hardly speak English. But I've been in the grocer's shop when she was there and she spoke just like you and me. A big order she had that day with wine and spirits. Someone must like a drop in that household. But of course she never thought of taking it away herself. Oh no — the messenger boy has to do that with his basket so full he could hardly push his bike, far less ride it. Sometimes she has visitors — ladies and gentlemen off the train and they drive up the West Water or have outings up the Glen. A foreign-looking lot. I wouldn't wonder if they were spies. Her name? A funny-like name. De Pass. It sounds French to me. *Miss* de Pass. But I'd be very surprised if she is still a Miss. For she's coming up to thirty. And she doesn't look like Miss anything to me. You can always tell. At least I can.'

The question must still have been how he could legitimately get in touch with her. Make contact. One evening he got so far as actually to start a letter to Miss de Pass for he had re-membered that the true name for the corncrake was landrail which *was* in his dictionary: râle de genêt. But he tore the letter up and burned the scraps in the fire. Once he cycled past towards the West Water and looked up to where the villa stood in its pines — a rather sombre building with overhanging eaves and a lot of woodwork painted dark green. But there was no one about except a man cutting the grass round a rustic summer house set in the lawn before the front door. A couple of weeks later, when the trees by the West Water were already turning colour, he went past again. This time there was a pony and trap by the front door. Two children — a boy and a girl of about thirteen or fourteen — ran out of the house and jumped into the trap. He waited as long as he could but had to move on. Looking back from beyond the end of the village he saw the trap come down into the road and drive off towards the station. There was a woman at the reins. He presumed it must be her.

It was on the following day that she appeared. It was just after half-past nine. They had taken the attendance and sung the morning hymn. Some of the children had brought little sheaves of oats, barley and wheat which stood on the window-sills in high glass jars. There was a slight stir as inkwells were filled and jotters distributed. Then the pupils bent over their desks and there was no sound except when one of them shifted their feet or a pen scratched the paper. He was walking up and down between the terraced desks looking over shoulders, encouraging, admonishing boys and girls who looked up sideways at him with a mixture of respect and apprehension. He was almost back at floor level when there was a tap at his door which caused all heads to rise together. 'Get on with your work now,' he said and walked over to the door. He could see no one through the glass panelling of the upper part of the door for whoever was there had drawn back momentarily out of sight.

When he opened the door she was standing there in a pose he had seen before, poking with her umbrella at the joints between the tiles in the corridor. 'Bonjour,' she said, 'est-ce que je vous dérange?' He hesitated a moment then gauchely asked her to step into the classroom where at a sign the pupils rose and chanted: Good morning, miss. She returned their greeting and remarked how well they behaved. He smiled with gratification and waited for her to explain her presence. To his astonishment she walked over to the blackboard. 'Ah, algebra,' she said, 'I used to love algebra. I did not expect to find it being taught here.' Perhaps she saw a trace of surprise and tenseness in his face for she apologized and proceeded to state her business, talking in a low voice. He listened, painfully aware that all over the classroom, and indeed in the next door room as well, all attention, including Miss Troup's — although she tried hard to conceal it — was focused on the pair of them as they talked. She, however, was apparently unaware of or indifferent to it, was relaxed, standing with one hand on the top of the fireguard along which she ran the tip of a gloved finger. The point was this: she had two children staying with her – children of a close friend of hers — who would be there for a few months. They needed someone to tutor them in English, Latin and mathematics. Would he consider undertaking the responsibility? They were not stupid — assez intelligents en effet — and he might not find the work too onerous or too boring. Perhaps he might want to think it over. She held out her hand with a frank gesture and turned to go. He opened the door and escorted her down the passage to the entrance. 'I have considered it,' he said as they reached the porch. 'I accept.' 'Bravo,' she said, 'I like people who show some decision. Here is my card. Perhaps you will let me know your terms and what time would best suit you. Au revoir, monsieur.'

He watched her go down the playground. She did not look back. He turned and went back to the classroom where the voices were rising in pitch and volume. As he walked in at the door they fell at once into a silence. 'No more chattering,' he said, 'woe betide anyone who has not finished by the end of the lesson.' He was still at times astonished by the way in which he could impose his authority on a class. 'Quos ego' he thought to himself and wondered whether she would have recognised and shared the Virgilian reference — the two words with which Aeolus, king of the winds, subdued the storms.

That evening he wrote in his best and most careful hand to Miss Elizabeth de Pass to inform her that he would be happy to undertake the tutoring of the two children. His fee was five shillings an hour, which he hoped might not appear excessive. Saturday morning would be the most suitable time for him. He remained hers faithfully etc.

Elizabeth de Pass. How to explain her presence in Slateford? How to construct her past? For the purposes of my romance I have given her H's looks, intelligence and directness, but I require other details which I shall take from someone else with another destiny than hers whom I knew much later.

She was born, such is my hypothesis, the daughter of a rabbi in Russian Poland. A rebellious adolescent, she was expelled from home; her father said Kaddish over her — the prayer for the dead. In St. Petersburg she found a post as governess in the family of a rich merchant, Jewish and of German origin. There were two young children to look after and an elder brother, Boris, handsome in his student's uniform, brave, and like herself, rebellious. He was a member of a Socialist club of about a dozen young men, most of them students at the Technological Institute — among them a short but robust young man from Samara, already bald with a fringe of reddish hair and a small beard. Ulyanov by name, his elder brother had been hanged at twenty-one for terrorist activities. It was no doubt inevitable that the two should fall in love and marry secretly. When the young man's mother discovered her anger was terrible. Then the son was arrested. Elizavyeta was received back into the household on tolerance while the mother desperately pulled strings at the Ministry of the Interior to buy her son's freedom. He was released but had to go abroad at once as a condition of liberty. He took his young wife with him to Austria, to Germany. There he left her almost without means and returned to Russia illegally. For a time she taught as a governess, was then an actress with an entrée into the intellectual society of Berlin where she was taken up and 'protected' by an industrial chemist from the Ruhr, a widower with two children and advanced political and moral views. In his company she came to Glasgow to an international exhibition, although she was far advanced in pregnancy. In Glasgow she miscarried. Her health deteriorated. His business affairs called him back to Germany. Through his Scottish agent he found her the village in Slateford, a village noted for its healthy climate (due, they said, to the ozone from the pine woods), supplied her with a generous allowance and hoped she might with time recover her health. To his children, who had now arrived on holiday, she was known as Tante Elizabeth. She was cultured, widely read in three languages, without religion.

I have given her the name of a family that used to come to the village for long periods when I was small: a woman with a son and daughter. Dark and foreign-looking, they were possibly Jewish but I do not believe that anyone in the village — certainly not my parents — had any concept of what was or was not a Jew. At all events they kept to themselves and were a source of mystery and speculation because although no one could possibly accuse them of giving any kind of offence they were in some quite specific way different. Once in winter, they appeared on skis in the village street and caused great though elaborately concealed excitement and comment. It is true that all 'visitors' were perceived as of a different species with different habits and customs from the village people — nannies, school uniforms, strange accents, unaccountable tastes for which the grocer catered and prospered thereby. But this family was even more markedly different and set apart from the others. I can still remember their faces and my curiosity.

Having decided to undertake this new assignment my father foresaw two difficulties. What to do about Jim Mitchell and how to intimate to Mrs Ramsay that he would henceforward be spending his Saturday mornings at the villa on the edge of the village; for tell her he must if only to avoid inquisitions. That she knew Miss de Pass had called at the school he guessed the moment he came back from work that evening. She did not beat about the bush but said, as she laid before him the black pudding that was his high tea, that she heard he had had visitors at school, the plural being a deliberate error, a calculated imprecision, to give an impression that her intelligence was much less accurate than in fact it was and force him to make a correction. He agreed that he had had a visit. The neutral noun was played as a check to her gambit. She had heard, she was forced to go on, revealing her true knowledge, that it was that Miss de Pass. She supposed she must have been wanting to see if there was a place in the school for these two children — whoever they belonged to — who were running wild in the woods and down by the West Water. He said No and then, after a moment's pause during which he speared the black pudding with his fork, added: 'She has asked me to tutor them at home. On Saturday mornings.' 'Fancy that now,' said Mrs Ramsay holding up her hands in surprise. 'Three people to tutor will be a lot.' The oblique reference to Jim Mitchell was a calculated embarrassment. He blushed slightly, took a mouthful of pudding to gain time and then remarked that he thought Jim Mitchell would manage without that much coaching this term. He had made real progress over the summer. 'They'll miss you at the mill,' said Mrs Ramsay meaningfully. Which was more or less what Mrs Mitchell said when he went over that same evening to disengage himself. Jim didn't need so much attention now that he was back at school. Maybe when the exams were a bit nearer he would help Jim with his revision. Of course they would be seeing him again. Mrs Mitchell was more specific than Mrs Ramsay: 'May will miss you,' she said with a significant inflection.

So, on the Saturday, having received through the post a note accepting his terms in what, from the superscription on the envelope, he recognized as a continental hand he set off down Church Street, conscious of Mrs Ramsay's eyes watching him from behind the curtains of the bedroom window, and turned up right towards the villa. He walked in at the gate without hesitation. On one side the ground fell away steeply into a tangle of wild raspberry bushes, now a brown autumnal tinge, with paths through them where no doubt the children ran wild. In the summer house there was a book lying on the bench. He wondered if it were hers and what it might be. For a moment he was tempted to go quickly across the grass to find out but instead continued on his way with his feet crunching loudly on the gravel as if to give warning of his approach; but no face appeared at any of the windows to see who this might be. He rang the doorbell. There was a long interval during which he wondered whether he had indeed heard it tinkle faintly at the back of the house. His hand was raised to ring again when the door was opened by a rather dumpy woman of fifty perhaps who without a word motioned to him to enter. Mutely she opened a door and ushered him into the drawing room which was solidly furnished. Above the mantelpiece hung a picture unlike any he had ever seen: a bright landscape with what might be snow and a church, a horse and a sledge, indicated in brilliant flashes of colour. He was still looking at the picture when he heard the door open and turned to see Miss de Pass enter with a child on either hand. She presented them — David and Rachel — and then asked: 'So you like it?' He was at a loss and replied that he didn't know. 'At least that's honest,' she said. 'Where would you like to work. Here or in the study.' It was curiosity to see more of the house as much as his feeling that a study might be better suited for teaching that made him opt for what was, he discovered, a rather small room at the back — originally perhaps a servant's bedroom but now largely occupied by a baize-covered table piled with books and periodicals, beside them an inkpot with a bright brass lid, a stone split open to show pale amethyst crystals and a small oval bowl of dark wood, carved to the shape of a bird, decorated with a curious formal pattern. What surprised him in the room was its bareness — the almost monastic sparseness of its furnishing and the whitewash of its walls on which there hung, just above the level of the table, a photograph of a woman in her thirties with a slightly pointed face and hair piled loosely on top of her head. No other pictures but delicate arrangements of pale dry grasses and dried flowers including one that must when plucked have been an extraordinary, intense blue. Much of this he was able to focus on only with time. Now with a word to the two children in some language he did not understand she left, closing the door — returned however almost immediately with a discreet knock and an apology to take from the table drawer what looked like a box of cigars. The children laughed; there was another brief exchange in the unintelligible language. The door closed and the lesson began.

'We will start with English,' he announced. 'Let me see how well you can read.' And he took out of his Gladstone bag a book and laid it on the table. 'Who will start?' There was a moment's hesitation. The boy looked resolutely down at his feet and made no sign of willingness but his sister volunteered. She began, hesitating over the dipthongs and feeling her way amidst the unfamiliar vowels.

I remember him as if it were yesterday, as he came plodding to the inn door, his sea-chest following behind him in a hand-barrow; a tall, strong heavy nut-brown man, his tarry pigtail falling over the shoulders of his soiled blue coat, his hands ragged and scarred, with black, broken nails and the sabre cut across one cheek a dirty lurid white.

'Good,' he said, interrupting her. 'Now you, David.' David began to read reluctantly; he flushed red at his uncertainties and struggled with an anger that at last burst out, causing him to rise abruptly from his chair and to run out slamming the door. There was a hush in which his sister sat composedly with her hands folded in her lap looking out of the window to the bare stubble fields behind the house. The tutor sat quietly too. He had restrained the flare of temper provoked by this rejection of his teaching and now reflected that this was going to be a different task from that of teaching the village children over whom his authority was so established. From the front of the house there came a noise of voices rising in argument in which a woman's — presumably that of the housekeeper — was prominent. He thought of the discipline to which he had had to bow as a boy that age in the Board School in Stirling and which he had inherited as part of his professional training. But these were privileged children to whom the harsh rules of ordinary education did not apply. The voices outside died down. The door opened and the boy sidled in and with a murmured apology took his seat. The mathematics lesson went more smoothly for the boy was adept at numbers and quick to construct the Euclidean figures in geometry. The teacher had barely drawn his watch to see whether it was near midday yet when there was a knock at the door and Miss de Pass came in. The children rose. The girl repeated the slight curtsey she had given in the drawingroom, the boy once more bowed slightly, stiffly. Then together they turned away and ran off down the corridor.

'I apologize for David's behaviour,' said Miss de Pass. 'He has certain problems with his father and anyone who seems to

57

take his father's place. There are some people, Mr Scott, who believe that we can attach universal validity to the legend of King Oedipus, whose destiny moves us so greatly because it might have been ours. I heard a remarkable lecture on the subject in Vienna. You are for these two or three hours *in loco parentis* — are you not? — in this house where women prevail. So you must expect to incur his antagonism occasionally.'

These were riddles he would carry away with him but meantime he followed her to the drawingroom where they sat to drink coffee — he did drink coffee? In this country it was difficult to know but he had been in France so she assumed he did — and eat a rich dark chocolate cake. 'Lienchen makes it herself – marvellously,' she explained, 'but so she should — she comes from Vienna.' Then with a sudden switch of subject she enquired what had taken him to Perpignan.

I do not know what took my father to Perpignan. Were there connections between his training college and the lycée there? Had the principal encouraged him, recommended him? Why Perpignan? I do not know. But to Perpignan he did go to act as a tutor in English at the lycée or — more probably and more lowly still — to be an usher, *un pion*, the object of half-understood jokes on the part of the boys and formal politeness on the part of the staff to whose homes he was never invited and whom he met socially only over a coffee in a cafe or outside in summer drinking pastis or a citron pressé (which he secretly preferred), while they watched the townspeople join with the greatest naturalness in the ever-widening circling movement of the *sardane* to the music of a trio: wind instruments of some sort and a drum. Once, I believe, from an odd reference of disgust, he had been persuaded to join a group of the younger, unmarried staff to drive to Céret, to the little bullring there, to see a corrida. The bull-fighters were no doubt *novilleros* — boys learning the danger skill, clumsy and

58

afraid, so that the bulls were stuck full as a pincushion of banderillas and swords until death came at last in choking gouts of blood. I believe that in Perpignan he lost both his virginity and his faith; but that is pure supposition and he never spoke to me of it nor to my mother: nor would I have expected him to do so.

As I write I am thinking of course of my real father who went not to Perpignan but to Angoulême, where I have no doubt his life was blameless — although that year was a blank in his history to which he never referred. But I have chosen Perpignan because of a summer spent there with someone now dead. There was a long, hot drive through the Midi followed by days in the Pyrenees and by the sea where one afternoon, playing with the sand, she lost the wedding-ring she still wore, and sieved the sand in vain for an hour in a state of guilt and misery. On the way north, on a sudden impulse, I drove through Angoulême curious to see the lycée as if I might somehow discover something about that blank year. But time was short and the lycée eluded me. In this fantasy into which I project him I sometimes imagine him like that gaunt figure in Vigo's film *Zéro de Conduite*, ruling a dormitory of boys with a clap of hands, sleeping in a curtained cubicle in the middle of the dormitory, crucified (symbolically) in his up-ended bed as the pupils march in procession through a blizzard of down and feathers from their torn pillowcases. That would suit one side of him. I would rather he were that other teacher in the film, the liberating spirit with about him some of the swagger of Charlot who engages in the children's struggle against oppression and absurd rules; but it would do too much violence to his austere nature to imagine that he could so unbend, so challenge authority. But at all events in a lycée I now place him.

Naturally he did not mention to Miss de Pass the loss of his faith or his virginity. She was in any case interested in questions

59

about which he knew little: the condition of the French peasantry, the state of local industry, the staple crops, the political situation. The teachers were, he could judge from their conversation, strongly anti-clerical, convinced of the need for the educational system and the teaching profession to stand as a bulwark of the Republic. Dreyfusites, she expected. Yes, he said, they talked a lot about Dreyfus. She looked at him quizzically and he was aware of having in some way exposed himself. Why? he wondered on his way home in a strange mood between excitement, annoyance and puzzlement, for — in spite of her apparent frankness and openness — there had been, he felt, something in her behaviour which set a distance between them, a kind of hauteur more intellectual than social — something very different from the condescension of Miss MacIllroy yet just as clear, or so it seemed to him. On the other hand there was her readiness to talk and discuss, to explain. Thus the blue flower amongst the dried grasses in the study was, he learned, a gentian, *gentiana lutea*, the dark flower of the Alpine meadows. He had not felt he could ask about the photograph so did not mention it. What impulse was it, he wondered, that led her to explain — perhaps to study his reaction — that this dear friend of hers, now a student at the Sorbonne, had been expelled from her lycée in Kharkov because she had led a rebellion against compulsory attendance at prayers and had set up a reading circle among the girls to study radical literature instead of the Bible. There was another enigma. Bearing in mind her talk of the corncrake and how it had kept her awake as a child, he had brought her as an offering, as it were, the French translation he had culled from his dictionary: râle de genet. He had made the offering on the doorstep as he was about to turn away. But she had accepted it casually as if she had forgotten their talk about how the bird's harsh call had stirred memories in her and turned quickly back into the house.

For lunch that day Mrs Ramsay, with what he recognized as considerable cunning, served him one of his favourite dishes — mince and savoury balls, dumplings of flour and suet — as if trading them for information on the villa, its occupants and furnishings. Her interrogation took her habitual form of a series of hypotheses on the model of: I expect the children were right spoilt brats or I expect the housekeeper waits on them hand and foot or I expect there must be a fair bit of money there somewhere. He replied cautiously, barely suppressing a growing annoyance as her suppositions continued. In any case, she said, producing the most damning theory of all, she wouldn't be surprised if they weren't Christians at all. Never in church. The children playing with a ball on the lawn in full view of the road on the Sabbath. Herself going about on a bicycle on the Lord's day too. Before he ever came to the village during the terrible snow last winter she had been seen on a Sunday near the railway where the land sloped down to the West Water running about with sticks tied to her feet as if it were not a day to be kept holy. Rising from the table as she cleared away the dishes, still speculating, still insinuating, he was surprised at the way he had excused and defended this strange, foreign woman whom — if he thought about it — he barely knew, but round whom in his own mind speculations were also crystallizing and giving rise to intense curiosity, an urgent desire to know more about her, more of her. He was aware of and troubled by the intensity of his enormous inquisitive desire which was, he both knew and did not know, for the knowledge frightened him, akin to that childish interest in the unknown, the mysterious quality of women, which had led him as a young boy to rummage among the dresses his mother worked on or to watch on one terrible occasion through a partly open door as a customer dropped her skirt to the floor and, stepping out of it to try on a new dress, had caught sight of his still, tense figure and strained face with its prying eyes. It was his mother who slammed the door shut just as it was his mother who, once the customer had gone, stormed at him, ordered him to go to bed and wait till she had time to take her hand to his bottom; which she did till he wept and begged her to stop. When she did it was to tell him how he shamed her, how wicked he had been and how merciful she was to chastise him herself instead of telling his father who would, as sure as she was alive, have taken his belt to him and not his hand. Perhaps it was that day which laid deep in his being the link between the secret which, in some terrible way, women carried about with them, and the twin reactions to it of guilt and an almost irresistible desire to see, to experience in some way not yet revealed to him that knowledge which must be the same knowledge as the text in Genesis talked about: the knowledge of good and evil, which was linked with the covering of nakedness. What else did the Bible mean when it said that Abraham or David or any other Old Testament hero 'knew his wife'? It was therefore with some tingle of excitement that he next Saturday walked up the drive to the door of the villa, which once again was opened by the housekeeper. There was no sign of Miss de Pass. The lesson passed off quietly. The children left him with their usual polite gestures and ran off laughing, whether at him, at some private joke or merely in relief that they were free once more he could not tell. The housekeeper let him out. The same ritual was repeated the following Saturday. He felt slighted and annoyed. But comfort came in the form of a letter bearing the postmark of Vienna. It enclosed a postcard of a giant wheel in an amusement park and a — as it seemed to him — repentant note apologizing for the fact that she had to leave suddenly on business. She hoped the lessons were going well and signed herself: Yours sincerely, E. de Pass. He did not know whether the 'sincerely' was a conscious choice rather than 'faithfully' or merely due to ignorance of the etiquette of letter-writing in English.

Next morning he shared the duty of supervising the collection at the church door with Mr Jameson, the village tailor, a distinguished white-haired man with a certain soft civility of manner derived, perhaps, from the need to placate customers like Miss MacIllroy and her brother. Their duties required them to be at the church early, almost as early as Willie Hamilton who, with a redness of eye more marked than usual, which caused Mr Jameson to suggest he had taken a dram too many the previous night, opened the door, carried the great bible up into the pulpit and laid out the minister's gown. Usually May Mitchell arrived as the doors were opened and instructed Willie what numbers to place on the indicator which told the congregation what hymns, psalms and paraphrases they were to sing that day. Usually my father was there to pass the time of day with her, to enquire after the health of her father and mother, to joke about Phemy's hypochondria, her latest fads and fancies, and to be informed of Jim's latest escapade. This morning for the first time he was too late to see May come into the church, slightly flushed from her mile-long walk from the mill so that by the time he arrived and laid his top hat in his pew she was already sitting at the organ running her fingers over the keys and looking down to check the movement of her feet on the pedals. The bell was ringing overhead; at the stroke of eleven from the clock on the village hall the ringing died away slowly although you could still hear the vibration of the bell. May struck up the voluntary: Handel's Largo in G. The congregation were slowly entering the church. Willie had taken up his post behind a curtain at the end of the organ away from the worshippers and was pumping at the bellows. The minister gravely mounted the steps to the pulpit, clasped his hands on his lectern in a posture of intense prayer, opened his eyes and announced the first paraphrase: O enter then his gates with praise, approach with joy his courts unto, Praise laud and bless his name always, for it is seemly so to do. Under the cover of the singing John Scott and the tailor walked quietly in, having counted the collection, and took their seats. It was with a sense of relief that the headmaster did so; he had avoided a direct meeting with May. No doubt they would see each other when the service was over and he must again, as an elder, stand at the door and watch the congregation leave. But that was an hour away. Meanwhile there was the sermon to sit through. The Reverend James Murdoch had at some time compiled a course of sermons on the Book of Ezekiel; it lasted six weeks and gave him an opportunity to rake over the fulminations of the apocalyptic text and relate them to the present state of the world, to lack of regard for the

Sabbath and to the undue emancipation of women. He announced the reading: The Book of Ezekiel, the thirteenth chapter and the seventeenth verse:

> Likewise, thou son of man, set thy face against the daughters of thy people, which prophesy out of their own hearts, and prophesy thou thus against them and say: 'Thus saith the Lord God: Woe to the women that sew pillows to all armholes and make kerchiefs upon the head of every stature to hunt souls.'

And again in the same chapter, verse twenty:

> Your kerchiefs also I will tear and deliver my people out of your hand, and they shall be no more in your hand to be hunted; and ye shall know I am the Lord. May God bless this reading of his holy word and to his name be the praise.
> The text for today is from this same book of Ezekiel: 'Likewise thou son of man, set thy face against the daughters of thy people, which prophesy out of their own heart.'

My father listened with little more than half his attention, wondered what Miss de Pass would have made of the strange text, looked across to where May sat until she caught his eye whereupon he looked away quickly and surreptitiously beneath the ledge of his pew began to draw Pythagoras' theorem on the flyleaf of his bible.

It had been boredom as much as anything else that predisposed him to agnosticism — the incomprehensible readings from the Old Testament prophets, the mystifications, the lack of answers to his boyish questions: what did it mean when it said Jesus healed a woman with an issue of blood; why was Onan killed for spilling his seed on the ground; what was a harlot? All questions avoided or rebuked. But above all what, as he grew older, he came to recognize as the desperate, grinding pedantry of the exposition of the texts, which went along with a brand of lachrymose piety and repugnant imagery that talked of being washed clean in the blood of the Lamb. He still shuddered, as he had as a child, to hear the line from the hymn that spoke of the 'fountain filled with blood drawn from Emmanuel's veins'. There had followed increasing scepticism about the historicity of the bible and the probability of miracles. But it was Jacques Lebrun, teacher at the lycée in Perpignan that provided him with arguments. With Lebrun he had, as I imagine it, a relationship that oscillated between attraction (in which there may have been an element of sexual attraction) and repulsion (which might well have been due to recognition, at some level, of that attraction). Lebrun must have been a little older than my father, a tall, lean handsome man with gangling arms and almond-shaped, brown slightly myopic eyes through which he peered out in a curious way as he expounded his views on politics, women and religion. From the first day he had begun with a stream of badinage, to interrogate 'notre petit écossais' about his tastes, his reading, his beliefs and why he did not wear 'la jupe' and play 'la cornemuse', flouncing about as he did so, squeezing an imaginary bagpipe sack under one arm (the wrong one) and miming exaggerated modesty as he sat down and tugged his imaginary kilt over his knees. It was an assault against which my father could bring up few defences, for he did not know how to counter it; fortunately he kept his temper. It was followed by others: an examination of his knowledge of Latin and the Latin classics, which he passed, and of Greek in which he failed through almost total ignorance. Then came a cross-examination on religious beliefs in the course of which Lebrun leant forward as if to receive a confession and encouraged 'son fils' to be honest and reveal all so as to earn remission of sins. Have you ever touched yourself, he asked, with sinful intent? Have you gone with bad women? Do you know who Tante Marie is? There followed a rattled benediction and the injunction to say a thousand Hail Mary's. Then with a laugh Lebrun patted his victim on the back, said he would introduce him to Tante Marie personally one day and took him off to drink pastis in the square.

What lay behind Lebrun's attachment to him, my father decided, was his passion for teaching, or rather for imparting and sharing knowledge; it did not matter greatly whether it was with the students of the lycée or this graduate of Glasgow University with precise but narrow education who needed to be made to open his mind to philosophy — Bergson, for instance — and to lose what was left of his faith. Renan was Lebrun's hero. Le petit écossais should read his autobiography, *Souvenirs d'enfance*, and then *La Vie de Jésus*. It would, said Lebrun, cure him for ever of superstition and make the reading of the Bible tolerable for a person of intelligence which, joking apart, his friend was. 'I speak,' he added, 'as one once designed for the priesthood. Je parle en connaissance de cause.' Our unshakeable anchor, he explained, must be a clear scientific view of a universe where no free will superior to that of man is active in any perceptible manner. Christianity presented itself as a supernatural fact. But through the historical sciences one could establish — in his view irrefutably — that this fact was not supernatural and that, indeed, there never had been such a thing as a supernatural force. We reject the miracle not by *a priori* reasoning — did his friend know what that meant? — but by critical or historical reasoning. We could prove without difficulty that miracles did not happen in the nineteenth century and that stories of miraculous events reputed to have taken place in their days were based on imposture or credulity. But the evidence on which the so-called miracles of the eighteenth, seventeenth and sixteenth centuries were based was feebler still; for the further removed one is the more difficult it is to furnish proof of a supernatural occurrence. To understand that one had to have the habit of textual criticism and historical method. Like Renan, he found that a close study of the Bible, while revealing historical and aesthetic treasures, also proved to him that the book was no more exempt than another ancient book from contradictions, inadvertencies, errors. It was, in his view, no longer possible to maintain that the Second Book of Isaiah was by Isaiah. As for the Book of Judith, it was a historical impossibility.

Their conversations were long and intense. They left my father with a residue of scepticism which in later life he concealed closely — as he concealed so much else, including his sorrows and his pain. If he lost his faith at Lebrun's hands it was because it had never been strong; the sermons he had had to listen to he had always judged intellectually contemptible; the doctrine expounded in the catechism he found obscure and implausible. 'Read *La Vie de Jésus*,' cried Lebrun. 'Meanwhile having caused you to lose your faith it only remains to cause you to lose your virginity.' But that was not yet.

At last the sermon was over. There now remained only a hymn and no doubt a prayer in which the Reverend James Murdoch would attempt to wring out of the deity a number of mercies which he, His servant, would allot to various causes and persons. Then came the benediction and the organ began to play something quite cheerful, as if May too felt relief at the end of the service, while the congregation rose, gathered up its bibles and hymn books, gloves and handbags and walked towards the door. There could be no escaping the meeting with May's parents, for both were there as well as Phemy and Jim; no doubt Mrs Mitchell would once again raise the question of tutoring but for weekday evenings he had an excuse: apart from the question of the dark and muddy road to the mill (yet May negotiated it every Wednesday for choir practices) there was the fact that he had received requests to start evening classes — the requests having come from ex-pupils, the junior clerk in the bank and other young men now employed in the neighbouring town as shop assistants and clerks and who wished to better themselves. They had asked for classes in mathematics and English. He had no alternative but to accept the task. But suppose someone in the Mitchell family were to suggest Saturday morning? How would he parry that suggestion? He could plead that it was his only remaining free time but it was likely that the whole village, including the Mitchells, knew that he had been hired by Miss de Pass to teach the strange children who lived with her. Mrs Ramsay would have seen to that. So it would perhaps be necessary to brazen it out. Fortune was with him. The Mitchells were apparently in some haste to get home and only Phemy lingered for a moment to say with an air of false innocence: 'Oh, John, have you heard – Jim's going to work at the stables on Saturday mornings — learning about motorcars and how to mend them. I thought you'd be pleased to know.' She ran off quickly to join her parents who had paused at the corner of the street to allow her to catch up. When at last May came to the church door with her music case in her hand her smile was wan and cool. Awkwardly they walked up the street together. Outside Mrs Ramsay's she said goodbye and walked swiftly off after the rest of her family. He felt, he had to admit to himself, a considerable sense of relief.

It must have been about this time that he had his first brush with the School Board. It met in the village hall in a cavernous committee room. Under the chairmanship of Major MacIllroy, who behaved like the lord of the manor, there sat the two ministers, coolly cordial to each other and invited turn and turn about to offer up the opening prayer before business started; a couple of big farmers — Mr Torrie of the Mains, who could boast that he worked twenty pair of horse, great feather-hooved Clydesdales, and Mr Keillor of Bogside, who had fewer horse but more head of cattle than the Mains; and the village grocer, a brightly ambitious middle-aged man who consciously cultivated a likeness to Lloyd George and professed Liberal opinions. The bank agent was also a member and secretary to the Board. If one could find the bound volume of the minutes, written up in the same fine hand with abundant flourishes as he used to draw up a draft or make an entry in his ledgers, they might read like this:

The minutes of the last meeting having been read and approved, the Chairman requested someone to move the first item on the agenda: potato holidays. Mr Torrie moved that the potato holidays should this year run from the first of October to the tenth of that month inclusive. Mr Keillor seconded. Mr Scott, the headmaster, expressed the view that ten days was a long break in the middle of the first term of a school year and that it was difficult to pick up again after such a long interruption, moreover the shortness of notice made it almost impossible to plan the curriculum effectively. The Rev. W.

Arnot stated that it had always been the tradition that the village school closed for potato holidays to suit the needs of the farming community to whom the village was beholden in so many ways. He therefore supported the motion. The Rev. J. Murdoch, while appreciating the difficulties to which the headmaster had referred, felt nevertheless, on balance, that the potato holidays must be determined by the dictates of Nature, which this year had caused the potatoes to ripen at the beginning of October, that moreover the holidays provided a healthy experience for the children, who would return to their desks refreshed: mens sana in corpore sano. Major MacIllroy, while not wishing to intervene in the debate, suggested that there was an important principle at stake: whether the headmaster had the right to decide what was best for the school and its pupils or whether, taking into consideration the needs of the community, the members of the Board were not best suited to make such judgements. He did not think it necessary to put the matter to the vote since the will of the Board had been clear. However, if the headmaster insisted he would put the matter to the vote. The headmaster said he did wish a vote to be recorded. In favour of the motion: 6; those against: 1.

On the way out the Major caught up with the headmaster and said with grim joviality: 'You were in a minority of one, headmaster. An honourable position. But you pushed us hard, young man. I hope you're not going to make life difficult for yourself or for us. Anyway come and have a dram just to show there is no ill-feeling.'

The headmaster thanked him but said he did not drink (which was not strictly true as we know from the incident with the mead). The Major turned on his heel with something like contempt.

For a couple of sessions his tutoring continued at the villa without his seeing Miss de Pass. Each time he approached the door it was with a flare of hope. Each time it was Lienchen who opened it for him and without expression showed him to the study, which was unchanged except that there were more journals about. As he waited for the children — he could hear

Lienchen summoning them from the bottom of the garden where they were feeding a couple of tame rabbits in their pen — he scanned the titles and the books on the table. They told him little for they were mostly in German and what he took, by the script, to be Russian. But one was lying on the top with an English title: *The Eighteenth Brumaire of Louis Napoleon*. He opened the first page and began to read: 'Hegel remarks somewhere that all facts and personages of great importance in world history occur, as it were, twice. He forgot to add: the first time as tragedy, the second as farce.' And then further down on the same page: 'Men make their own history, but they do not make it as they please; they do not make it under circumstances chosen by themselves, but under circumstances directly encountered, given, and transmitted from the past.' Then the children came in with their customary half-curtsey and stiff bow. Across the fields he could see in the distance the potato-digging machine advancing slowly down the drills, the pronged wheel of the machine loosening and throwing up the potatoes and uprooting the shaws, while behind them came the long lines of women and children who with wet cold fingers and bent backs picked the crops from the heavy red soil; after them came the foreman to check that the drills had been picked clean. From time to time during the lesson he glanced up to watch the progress of the harvest and found himself wondering what use there was in the effort he made to teach boys and girls whose fate it was to hire themselves for such labour up and down the Great Strath. The thought was still in his mind when he dismissed the children. He stood for a minute looking out of the window and then took up the book once more to look at the opening paragraph. A step in the corridor made him lay it down in confusion. 'I beg your pardon,' he said, 'I was looking at this book.' Miss de Pass was unruffled. 'You should read it,' she said, 'One of my favourite pieces,' and she quoted: 'The tradition of all the dead generations weighs like a nightmare on the brain of the living.' Then almost sharply: 'Why do you laugh?' 'I was thinking that something like that was going through my own head.' 'A propos de quoi?' she asked. 'A propos of potatoes,' he replied and it was her turn to smile. 'Come and have a cup of coffee and tell me the connection between Louis Bonaparte and potatoes.'

Over the dark chocolate cake he told her about the School Board meeting, rehearsed the various interventions and imitated the Major so that she began to laugh. 'Ah, the Major,' she said. 'When I came here first his sister, Miss MacIllroy, left cards — is that right? — and then drove off with her pony before I could get to the door to greet her. Then I was invited to lunch on a Sunday. La cuisine anglaise I could endure but the conversation afterwards was impossible. I do not think I was rude but I was angry about British rule in India.' She laughed. 'They have not asked me back and Miss MacIllroy cuts me — that's what you say, isn't it?' When they came to discuss the meeting, however, although she praised his determination to place his dissent on record she cross-examined him sharply on his grounds for that dissent. Was it sufficient to attack the concept of potato holidays from the narrow view of pedagogy? She brushed aside an attempted explanation on his part and stated categorically: 'There is another more valid and concrete reason why you must oppose the idea. It is that these farmers are exploiting both your pupils and their mothers. There is today no good reason why any human being should have to perform such tasks. But so long as there is profit to be made out of manual labour the profit-makers will extract it rather than invent more humane ways of collecting crops. In the United States and Canada they already have farm machinery that can reap and — what is the word? — thresh corn in the same process. There is no reason except greed on the part of the farmers to explain the use of child labour, which is bad for the children *and* bad for education. I find that you did not formulate the question properly.'

He was not used to hear a woman speak like this, with such confidence and directness, without airs and graces — as his mother would say — demanding to be answered as an equal. His reply was undermined internally by the doubts he had felt

71

shortly before about the usefulness of his profession in this place and at this time; but he put it as persuasively as he could, going over the democratic tradition in Scotland, the long history of popular education dating back to the Reformation whereby every parish had had its school for centuries, the concept of the 'lad o' pairts' — what was that? she asked sharply; the bright boy, he interpreted — and the chance that some might have as others had had in the past (like himself, he added) to escape from the plough, the pit or the factory, and live a better life here or in Canada, America, South Africa, Australia. It was an argument he had often heard and he knew, he believed, how to marshal it. She listened with attention. This time she had no umbrella to play with as she listened and thought but he noticed how her forefinger felt the rim of the low table by her knee as she waited for him to finish.

'I agree. Some of these — what did you call them? — lads of parts will break out. Become teachers like you, ministers of religion, engineers, technicians, civil servants, but they will have broken out only to become the prisoners of another set of circumstances. They will be received into another social class but only on condition that they defend that class and its interest — against the people and the class among whom they were born.'

He had heard people talk in terms of class before; but they had never convinced him. Not that he was unaware of class distinctions — but he thought they could be exaggerated. He said as much and queried the concept.

'Let us be concrete, then,' she said. 'What class do you belong to? I know what class I come from. I reject that class. And I know what class I must support. The working class. You may not think so looking round this house, seeing the way I live and the way I dress. But I know where I stand. What about you?'

He hesitated. Did she expect him to explain about the tenement with its close smell, the stairhead lavatory, the wire handles of the milk-pails biting into his fingers as he delivered milk on winter mornings to earn a couple of shillings, about his drunken father and his mother, bitter with too much work and too little money, too many pregnancies and too many miscarriages or abortions.

'Let me guess,' she said. 'I would put you very close to the working-class — too close to them to feel comfortable. In other words, they represent for you what you might have been. There but for the grace of God, didn't someone say? So you have climbed, pulled yourself up through the educational system. With some effort because I'm sure it's not as simple, even for a' lad o'pairts' (did I get it right this time?) to break through. But what is the use of an educational system that skims the working class of its best brains and what is the use of these bright young men if they are not prepared — once they have broken through the system — to fight to make the opportunity universal, open to their class, not just to a few individuals in it?'

He began to talk: about his uncle who had gone deaf because of the clangour of the steam hammers in the mill where he had worked all his life and about his uncle's wife — a little woman of indomitable humour who wore a man's cap and a shawl except when she went visiting or to church. Of the periods of poverty when his father had no work, or did not look for it, but sat about the house in deep depression and what they ate was bread and dripping. She listened and then said:

'You see — you do know what I am talking about. About class. But you will forget — in ten years you will have forgotten. The village will tame you and claim you. Unless you fight — unless you make an effort.' She broke off and was silent for a moment then added with a smile. 'No doubt you will think me rude. But I am used to men and women who speak their minds and do not take offence. I hope you will not — take offence.'

At the door they shook hands in the continental way he had learned in France and had then had to unlearn on coming home. She had enjoyed their talk, she said. She was sorry she had been away for a couple of weeks — in Vienna. Someone she was very fond of had been passing through and they had to meet. On his way home he laughed to himself and wondered how the Reverend James Murdoch would judge this woman who 'prophesied out of her own heart' — speculated too about who it might have been that she was very fond of and who had been passing through Vienna. There were two strange concepts here: that people could, as it were, casually 'pass through Vienna' and that it was possible to speak so casually almost of being very fond of a person. What did that mean? Did it mean that she was in love with someone? Or was it perhaps merely a relation? Was it a man or a woman? Could a woman be very fond of another woman or a man for that matter? How did people who were 'very fond' of each other behave to one another? He knew that there was a stage in life, he had recently been passing through it, one might say, when people were said to be 'courting' and he remembered with a twinge the summer days at the mill but after the courting came marriage, which was a serious business and one in which, as far as he could see, there was not much space or time left for being fond of one another. He remembered the girls from his class at school — how they bloomed briefly, walking in groups on the High Street on a Saturday or strolling on the castle esplanade to watch the garrison's pipe band beat tattoo; how they had gone courting on the banks of the river Forth, sometimes with the stocky kilted privates of the Seaforth Highlanders, who were bold, brash and dangerous — or so his sisters said; how they had got married, some — as everyone at the church door knew — because they had to, some as the result of what seemed bewildering choices; and how when he came back from University and then from France he had seen them pushing their prams up to the Co-op, perhaps pregnant again, so different that he barely recognized them beneath the marks of housework, life in a tenement up three flights of stairs and constant demands of children and husbands. He was not aware that anyone had ever, in the sense she seemed to mean, been 'fond' of him. His mother had cared for him, bullied him, beaten him, pushed him upwards and away from his origins which she, being the daughter of a small farmer somewhere in the Lothians, who had married beneath her, despised. With his brothers and sisters he had fought and played but he had not felt fond of them — except perhaps for the brother nearest to him with whom he had shared the same punishments or invented subterfuges to escape chastisement by one parent or another; but their ways had diverged. He had emigrated to Canada, seldom wrote and when he did the letters said little except that it was cold in winter in the plains of Alberta, that there was a great future over there and that the best thing would be to chuck the old country and come over, cold or no cold.

His older brother, Tom, the one in the London shipping company, he was less close to — indeed felt uneasy with. He had experienced that sense of unease when last they met, when — he smiled involuntarily at the thought — he had been 'passing through London' on his way back from Perpignan. To find him he had to make his way across Tower Bridge and so down to the offices and warehouses overlooking the Pool of London. He had difficulty with the buses, taking one in the wrong direction originally, and then finding himself caught up by the docks in the turmoil of the drays with their great trampling hooves, the shouts of the dockers, the intense activity in which all these men and animals had a place and a purpose which was obscure to him. His brother he found at his desk by a window that gave on to the river. The Pool was packed with freighters moored stem to stern. On their decks brown sailors with bare feet and turbans were moving about purposefully while the cranes hoisted bales of merchandise from the holds and swung them on to the waiting lorries.

'Right,' said his brother to a couple of other spick-and-span young clerks, 'I've got to take my wee brother out to see the sights of London.' 'Don't let him do nothing you wouldn't do yourself,' one of them shouted after him and his brother laughed. 'Cheerio,' he shouted back. 'Chin-chin. I'll keep him away from Number Sixty-Nine.' The laughter died behind them as they ran down the wooden staircase and into the lanes between the warehouses where the derricks hoisted the bales into the storerooms and a squat engine came puffing past an inter-section. They ate in a crowded eating-house with wooden benches and long tables. His brother had a glass of ale with his steak and kidney pudding. My father asked for water. 'I thought you'd have been knocking back the wine a la frangsay,' commented his brother. 'How were the mademoiselles anyway?' The waitress had greeted him as an old acquaintance with 'Hello ducks' and was introduced as Liz. 'Going roller-skating tonight, then?' asked his brother. 'Bring a friend. I've got to look after little brother till tomorrow. Just back from France,' he added with a significant wink. But they didn't go roller-skating — went instead to Leicester Square to the Alhambra where his brother insisted he must see the chorus 'although I expect you've been watching them do the can-can in gay Paree.' They sat in the gods. Below, in the stalls, they could see the young men in evening dress who, his brother informed him, pinched the prettiest girls from the chorus line — 'mostly Jew boys too' he added with a touch of indignation. My father wondered at the term. To him a Jew was a remote concept which had significance only in the context of the Old Testament. So far as he knew, before he went to France he had never met one in all his life, would not know what one looked like and was astonished that it was as easy to identify them as his brother suggested. The concept was so remote that the arguments he had heard in the cafes of Perpignan over the Dreyfus affair — arguments which seemed to him marked by extraordinary and uncalled for vehemence — had puzzled him greatly but which revolved round the fact that this French officer, Dreyfus, court-martialled and imprisoned on Devil's Island, was a Jew. There had been, he felt, in the way Lebrun and his colleagues discussed the matter an element of inexplicable drama from which he was glad to be genuinely detached.

After the show they pushed their way through the promenade where the young gentlemen and the whores, young and old, jostled, bartered and joked, to stroll in Leicester Square and 'look at the talent' as his brother put it. When they at last made their way back to his brother's digs near Kings Cross my father had an intuition that but for his presence Joe's evening would have ended differently. For a moment he had it on the tip of his tongue to ask Joe the question which lay oppressively at the back of his mind and would wake him with a start to lie in a pool of sweat as he wrestled with the strange dreams that cloaked his fears. But the question remained unspoken. Next morning he caught the express from Euston to Glasgow. The moment had passed.

Now as he lay down in his bed at Mrs Ramsay's and thought back over his conversation with Miss de Pass and wondered at the twinge of what he recognized as jealousy over her talk of someone she was 'fond of', the fears returned. He still, he reflected with a new sharper fear, did not know the answer to the question that was fixed like a barb in his mind.

It is not difficult to imagine the reasons for the troubling guilts that followed my father to Slateford. His sexuality and his experience of sex was something that he must have found it almost impossible to discuss with any living creature. He belonged to a culture which was ruled by an extraordinary ambivalence about sex and sexual mores. It was not possible to grow up, as he did, in a tenement or to go through the kind of schools in which he spent his childhood and early youth without being aware of certain truths of physiology and of sexual practices or without absorbing — especially within the domain of his mother's jealous protection — a fear of a terrible force, of which he was already conscious, that could apparently cause boys and girls, not to mention grown men and women, to take leave of their senses and abandon the standards of decent 'clean' living. As he grew older his mother increasingly warned him in terms he half-understood to keep away from the bad women who lay in wait out there to seize upon innocent youths like himself. It was a topic which the boys at school discussed with a mixture of ignorance and knowingness using the basic terms of a vocabulary which each one of them knew but which each one again knew to be tabu. Anyone caught using them was certain to be thrashed and disgraced by parents or by teachers. But what other language was there to talk in? What could one call the organs of sex, how describe the obscurely guessed at act of love, of mating, as one enquired genuinely, innocently, fearfully, into the problems of adolescence and tried to cope with its impulses, terrors and secret pleasures? When he left for Perpignan he was, I believe, still a virgin. Some of the boys in the highest grade at school might boast of the extent to which they had explored the anatomy of the two or three girls who were known to lend themselves to such investigations. At university and training college there had been others who hinted at more advanced knowledge and even of experience; but on the whole the rigours of the social conventions under which they had been brought up had to be endured until the wedding night when that which lay hid would be made plain. But what was that precisely? Once greatly daring he had framed a question to his mother which hinted at his curiosity. She replied confusedly but conveyed the impression that it was a dirty business and, turning to the sink, clattered with her pots and pans.

In Perpignan he must have found himself in a different climate. He had been instructed by the Principal of his training college that he would be well advised to seek out the Eglise Protestante, which would no doubt exist, hidden away rather like a Catholic chapel in a solidly Protestant country town in Scotland, and to attend 'le culte' each Sunday; it would, apart from anything else be excellent for his French to follow the sermon. Failing this there might be the danger of being exposed to the temptations of the Roman Church whose members were notoriously lax in morals and in belief, with no real knowledge of the Scriptures; moreover it was common knowledge that confession, that farcical ritual, permitted them to commit whatever sins they chose and then by the mechanical repetition of religious formulae to find forgiveness — 'for you understand there is no such thing in the Church of Rome as a true prayer, that spontaneous wrestling with God in order to obtain his forgiveness which is the mark of the true Christian, be he layman or minister of the Gospel.' It followed from this that the French nation was deeply marked by vices of all kinds, some of them unmentionable, and that he would be well advised to avoid the company of any young fellows — colleagues at the lycée perhaps — who were given to such lewd and vicious ways. But in Perpignan there was no Eglise Protestante and the congregation of the Catholic Church seemed to an outward glance sober and not obviously depraved. It is true that when he ventured into the cathedral during Mass they seemed oddly casual in their behaviour, coming and going at all times through the service, even moving around to stand at the back of the nave, so that only the little tinkle of the bell when the host was elevated brought a true sense of religious attention. He had found the experience curious and slightly disturbing for he had not known how to behave — whether to imitate the late-comers and dip a finger in the holy-water stoup, whether to genuflect as he passed in front of the altar. On the other hand, no Presbyterians could have been stricter in their morals than the two maiden ladies with whom he lodged, whose cuisine was excellent, their furniture extraordinarily rickety and their toilet arrangements more primitive than the stair-head closet he had grown up with. Although they themselves clearly had little or no experience of the phenomena they described they were fiercely condemnatory of what they saw as the moral decline of the Third Republic under the influence of freemasons, Jews (again) and Socialists like Jaurès whose name made them blanch and reach for their rosaries. It is true that at the weekend he saw soldiers with the garrison walking out with girls who, by their behaviour, reminded him of some of the girls from his own tenement. Giggly, disputatious, strident, dressed with a bravado that was an attempt to conceal their poverty, they might, he recognized, be the kind that 'let one see'. But it was no different in Stirling where the Argyll and Sutherland Highlanders walked the girls by the banks of the Forth or the Allan Water or at fair time took them on the switchback or the big swings where they laughed and screamed and showed an occasional flash of white petticoat or black stockings, the almost subliminal glimpse of a thigh. One of the girls in his street had had a baby from a soldier who went off in the trooping season to India or Hong Kong and left her with her belly full; no doubt the same might happen if the *chasseurs* were ordered off to Indo-China or Tonkin or Madagascar or to fight the Riff tribesmen in North Africa. So it seemed to him there was little to give between the two communities. It was only some months after his arrival that he learned that there was another side to the placid, well regulated life of the town, its solid respectability, although retrospectively he thought he ought to have had some suspicion that all was not as it appeared in the surface. Had not Flaubert called that chronicle of sexual transgression, *Madame Bovary*, an account of *les moeurs de province?*

This is how he came to learn about some of the other moral customs of provincial Perpignan.

It was just after Easter and so in his last term at the lycée. In his digs he had endured Lenten fare, for his landladies made no concessions to heretics. The weekend after Passion Sunday they were sitting in a café — himself and two or three of the younger members of staff. What they asked him, half-mockingly, had he abjured for Lent? Falling in with their joke he told them of his meagre meals and the enforced asceticism in the weeks preceding Easter. But what else? asked Lebrun, for whom, as I have indicated he felt an attraction that was accompanied by a certain unease — a sense that in his company he must be wary, for he was full of witticisms, of repartee and of outrageous statements masquerading as mere common-sense with which he entrapped the innocent or the inattentive. He was famous for his imitation of M.le directeur, whose cough and quick darting glances behind the pince-nez that perched on his rather large reddish nose he could reproduce perfectly, just as he could imitate the directeur's voice, rather tight and nasal, as it intoned an alexandrine from Racine, preferably spoken by a female character, like:

Madame, ou je me trompe ou durant vos adieux
Quelques pleurs repandues ont obscurci vos yeux.

The voice swooped and fell; a hand beat the rhythm of the verses. Round the café table his listeners would laugh and throw themselves back in their chairs so that the billiard players stopped their game and demanded silence which would be observed for a moment or two only to be broken by renewed laughter as Lebrun ordered a pernod with a couplet that had a marvellous resemblance to the kind of lines that were Racine's stock-in-trade for linking scenes. That evening Lebrun's post-Lenten spirit was not to be restrained. So, what else had M.l'écossais, deprived himself of? He did not smoke so that could be eliminated. He barely drank — a glass of wine now and then, watered. But what about the other pleasures of the flesh? John Scott flushed and was silent. Rising suddenly in his chair Lebrun hunched his shoulders like M.le directeur leaning over his desk to castigate a pupil and declaimed: 'I must state without equivocation that I have known students of a certain brilliance, students destined indeed for a career at the Ecole Normale, to which my colleagues and I have directed the talents of more than one illustrious pupil — I have known, I say, students of a certain brilliance who have failed the ultimate challenge of the entrance examination. Why? Not because they had not mastered the curriculum, not because they lacked native intelligence but because they had dissipated their energies, drained their vital force, if I may be allowed a reference to a great philosophical thinker, by practices which — were I a believer — I would categorize as equivalent to the sin against the Holy Ghost but which — as a mere layman — I would define as a pollution of young bodies as fatal as the attentions of the succubus. The noun, you should note has a masculine form but designates a female being, the voluptuous creation of overheated minds and enervated and abused bodies. Let these words be a warning to you all.' There was a round of applause from the table which made Madame look up from her washing of glasses and smile indulgently. 'So, M.l'écossais, let that be a warning to you too. Unless that is to say you have been sampling the charms provided by Tante Marie.' John Scott did not know how to respond. So he smiled uncertainly and looked at the wine left in the bottom of his glass. 'However,' Lebrun went on, 'if that is not the case and since Holy Week is now over and with it all the superstition and mumbo jumbo that accompany it I have a proposal: mihi est propositum ire ad puellas. On va rigoler un peu — tu entends, mon cher écossais?' And he took my father by the arm, laid the price of the drinks on the table, bowed to Madame and swept out declaiming: 'Chez Tante Marie, chez Tante Marie.'

Tante Marie's was in a quiet part of the town, down a narrow street, a close they would have called it in Stirling, at the end of which there was a tall house with persiennes tightly closed and a peephole in the door through which, when Lebrun rang, an eye peered out to scan the group of young men on the pavement. When the door opened there was a waft of warm air, heavy with tobacco smoke, smelling of something else which John could not identify but which was, in fact, the smell of warm, perfumed naked human flesh. A middle-aged woman in black with a blunt pug-nosed face and long jet earrings came towards them. Lebrun greeted her with mock reverence, introducing to her holiness, Tante Marie, friends of his some of whom she no doubt knew already — as did her nuns — and a friend and colleague of his from la belle Ecosse where such temples as that where Madame reigned were apparently unknown. He hoped she would treat him with respect due to a colleague from the lycée and also a foreigner who would doubtless take back with him reports about the establishment to his native land. Then he whispered a few words in her ear. With a laugh Tante Marie held out her hand to the stranger. It was short and pudgy and heavy with rings. 'Venez donc, monsieur,' she said in a voice that implied a command and walked ahead of him through a door shielded by thick velvet curtains beyond which, in a room lined with mirrors, John Scott was confronted by seven or eight naked women, some sitting on the plush settees that lined the walls, some standing in a small group, talking and smoking and laughing. When he entered in Tante Marie's wake they turned towards him and smiled; a couple of them rose from their settee and came to join the group which now formed a circle round him. Tante Marie, in what he knew was the flat accent of Marseilles, asked what his preference was: blonde or brunette — or there was a red-head. Where, she asked, was Fifi? A girl pointed upstairs. 'Ah,' said Tante Marie, 'a pity — I think she would have appealed to you. So, monsieur, the choice is yours.' John was dazed by these breasts, these hips and the dark or blonde triangles of hair in the shadow of the girls' thighs and stood in a kind of numb indecision. Suddenly one of those who had been sitting on the settee — a young girl with long hair hanging over her thin negligee, black hair that seemed to gleam with oil, and dark nipples on her large breasts stepped forward and took his hand. 'Allons, minou,' she said, 'on va monter?' He made to withdraw his hand but she had it tight in her grip so that, with a mixture of fear and mounting excitement, he was constrained to follow her up the stairs and into the corridor above. The room she led him to was at the far end. As they passed he saw that in some rooms the door was shut and a red light burned above the lintel; in others the door was open so that he could see beds, mirrors, towel rails and curious low kidney-shaped basins set on a stand. 'I am Dolores,' she said as she shut the door behind them, 'I am from Spain. You have had a Spanish girl before? Somos muy lindas.' John did not reply but stood and looked around him. Above the head of the bed, which was not so much a bed as a wide couch set close to a mirror that covered one wall, was an image of some saint that looked as if it had been cut out of an illustrated paper. A twig of palm was stuck behind it — a relic of Easter. Dolores lay down on the couch. Her legs were drawn up and slightly parted so that he was aware of a dark shaggy patch between her thighs. He still made no move. Dolores gave him time, saying hers was a nice room and pointing to the postcards stuck round the mirror of the dressing table which stood against the opposite wall. Above it was a picture postcard of some port: 'Malaga,' she said. 'I am from Malaga.' John still hesitated. The girl was still patient. 'Is he a baby then?' she said in a curious childish voice, 'Does he want Dolores to take his clothes off for him?' John let her undo his jacket and his waistcoat, then his shirt. Her fingers touched the skin of his chest and he shivered slightly. She ran her hand over his back as she began to unfasten his trousers. 'Allons, let's see what we have here.' His erection was proud with blood, intolerably naked. Her fingers touched his penis lightly so that he shut his eyes with tension; he could feel the rhythm of his breathing change and felt a flush spread — or so it seemed — from his sex to his chest and face. 'Does he want to visit Dolores?' she asked and peremptorily drew him close to the couch. 'Come,' she said. 'But first we must put a little coat on him. Une capote anglaise,' she laughed at the coincidence. The rubber was tight on his flesh. 'Now,' she said, 'we make him a little moist so that it is easier for him and for Dolores.' His eyes were shut. He was aware of warmth and pressure on his penis. opening his eyes he looked down and saw she had taken it between her lips. At that moment orgasm shook him, exploded in his skull and set his heart pounding. 'Ah,' said Dolores, considering the semen caught in the loose rubber at the tip of his penis, 'quel dommage. Mais ça sera pour une autre fois.' John was helpless. 'Come on,' said the girl, 'get dressed. Look, I'll take it off for you. Now wash yourself. There's water in the ewer.' He washed quickly and dressed, fumbling awkwardly at the buttons. Dolores meantime lay on the couch with her negligée wrapped round her, lit a cigarette and hummed a tune with a long wavering melodic line under her breath. She was withdrawn as if he were not there, yet a minute or two ago she had touched his most intimate being. 'Right,' she said swinging her legs on to the floor, 'down we go. You are going to give me something at least.' John searched in his trouser pockets and produced a franc piece. She laughed with a hint of contempt, spun the coin into the air, caught it and laid it on the dressing table. 'Some people are generous,' she commented. He did not know whether she meant it or not. At the bottom of the stairs Lebrun was chatting with a couple of girls, an arm round each naked waist. Dolores joined them. John saw them whisper together, saw them look round at him and then saw how Lebrun burst into laughter and cried out: 'Eheu, ejaculatio praecox. What a waste!' Then he took Dolores by the hand and ran off up the stairs. At the door John felt Tante Marie looking at him curiously. He was aware that there must be some fee, some tribute to Circe, as it were. But when he felt for his wallet Tante Marie smiled and said: 'M. Lebrun has already paid.' An elderly woman stood by the door, guardian of the peephole. She opened it for him and wished him bonsoir.

How often did John return to that close, walk past, looking up at the shuttered windows which hid images that he recalled with a kind of astonishment when he lay on his bed in the hot evenings in June and listened to the voices in the street and the sound of the bugles calling the last soldier back to barracks? Once or twice he got so far as to walk up to the door but each time his resolution failed as he was about to ring the bell. He wondered if the old woman — Tante Marie herself even — had watched him through the spyhole and mocked his faint heartedness, before going back to the room where the girls gossiped and waited and joined in the laughter, Once, in the market, where he had gone to buy cherries, he thought he saw Dolores with another woman. He edged closer to them but the two women turned away without seeing him and were lost in the press round the stalls, What lingered, along with the astonishing memory of women's bodies, was his fear — a double terror: on the one hand, a conviction that he had in some way defiled himself morally, made himself unacceptable to any decent girl; on the other, and more terrifying even, was the thought that he might — how he did not rightly know — have contracted some terrible disease, one of those he had heard men talk of and joke about in a way that concealed fear. But the manifestation of such a disease was a mystery to him.

In the lycée he surreptitiously consulted Larousse but the descriptions of venereal disease were too vague to satisfy his curiosity. Anxiously he examined his body and his penis, looking for he did not know what, convinced that a spot on his face, a pimple on his groin where he had pulled out a hair was a symptom of some unimaginable illness that would ferment in his body, break its way out in a plague of pustules and finally destroy his brain. Lebrun had lent him *Les Fleurs du Mal*. In it he read with startled interest Baudelaire's vision of Cytherea, Venus' island, that banal Eldorado of old rakes on whose shores a castrated body showed how one must pay for the sins of the flesh; then he too felt 'the long bitter river of grief rise into his mouth like vomit' and was moved like the poet to pray to be given the strength and the courage to look at his heart and his body without disgust. De contempler, he repeated to himself, mon coeur et mon corps sans degoût. It was a line that would spring to mind again and again with horror and yet with fascination at the shift in vowel sound from *coeur* to *corps*, so obvious and yet so mysterious in its effect; magic linked to fear.

Jacques Lebrun he avoided as far as possible after the visit to Tante Marie. At the end of June he packed his tin trunk and set out on the hard wooden seats of a slow train for the Channel and home. He kept up no links with Perpignan.

What was Lebrun's likely destiny? To be pounded into the mud at Verdun, scythed down by machine gun bullets on the Somme, drowned in a shell-hole in Champagne. No doubt I have passed some war memorial in a village of Northern France bearing his name. Above the plaque stands an impossibly dramatic *poilu* caught in the moment of death in the arms of some female figure that is perhaps an angel, perhaps merely an incarnation of the Republic. Or unwittingly I have driven past a war cemetery where he lies among the crosses that range themselves in diagonals and lines, immense perspectives of mortality, beside the roads where I went searching for the burial place of a dear friend killed in that other war of which I was a part.

One Saturday, having sent a note to Miss de Pass to say that he was unavoidably prevented from attending to tutor the children that morning, but would, if it suited her, come in the afternoon instead, he set off to visit the doctor in the nearest market town. After breakfast he mounted his cycle for a long ride against the wind that whipped the last leaves from the beech trees and drove showers of rain into his face. As he changed gear and pedalled strongly or, dismounting, pushed the bicycle up the long hill just a mile from the town's end, he wondered how he might find words to describe his case or make concrete his fears. He was early for the consulting hour in spite of the wind and had to spend time walking round the town, looking in the stationer's window before enquiring whether a book had arrived, visiting the cathedral with its round tower, a refuge from ancient wars, from rape, pillage and slaughter. When at last the clock in the High Street had got round to 9.30 he entered the waiting-room. There were others there before him: a pregnant woman with a baby in her arms, who was probably a tinker's wife, her legs scorched from sitting at camp fires on cold heaths; a father with his son — the boy's face was pitifully swollen with a gumboil — and a young married woman who, when the doctor called a name through the half-open door of his consulting-room, rose with great nimbleness and glided through the door with her eyes on the floor. She emerged a few minutes later, still collected, still downward-looking, and quietly left the room. It was the turn of the tinker-woman next; her baby tugged at a nipple and protested at being separated from it as the mother rose. From inside the consulting room the wail of the baby mingled with

the voice of the doctor and the woman's as they rose in pitch
and volume. Very soon the door was thrown open and the
woman emerged shouting that she knew her rights, that the
bairn needed something, that she could pay as well as the next
body, that she hadna heard him shout at the young lady. There
was a pause after she left as if the doctor required to regain his
equilibrium — indeed it was with conspicuous calm that he
summoned the boy and his father. Their business was soon
done. A yelp came from the boy who emerged almost at once
spitting blood into a handkerchief. 'Well,' said the doctor as
John Scott sat down, 'what can I do for Mr Scott?' He was a
man in his fifties with a white, nicotine-stained moustache, a
fiery face and prominent blue eyes. Behind his desk hung a
brown photograph of a group of officers posing in front of an
ambulance with a red cross prominent on its canvas hood; a
couple of turbanned Indian grooms held the heads of the mules
harnessed in the shafts. 'Well,' said John, and his mouth dried
as he spoke, 'I am afraid I may have caught an infection.'
'Infection,' barked the doctor, 'what kind of infection?' John
made a vague gesture towards his genitals. 'Ah, I see,' said the
doctor. 'Let's hope it's clap and not that other very nasty thing
— old syph. Let's have a look then.' As John shamefacedly
fumbled with his trouser-buttons the doctor continued to
ruminate. 'Never knew a gentleman yet that didn't have clap
at least once in his life. Mind you the Jocks out in India — that
was a problem. Some of them, I used to say, would put their
pricks where I wouldn't put my cane.' He laughed to himself
and taking a ruler from his desk lifted up John's penis for his
inspection. 'Pull back the foreskin, will you? That's a good
man. Where did you say you had this contact? Ah la belle
France: When? Six years ago? You've taken a long time to
come haven't you? Getting married, eh? Frightened you'll
give some nice girl the pox? You can pull your trousers up.
Short arm parade's over. Now then. Any gleet? Any discharge
then or now? Any sores, chancres, lesions? If you ask me all
you've had is a dose of the frights. But take this — three times a
day after meals. Cleans out the old waterworks. Otherwise as

sound as a bell, you'll be relieved to know — as sound as a bell.'

John muttered his thanks and found sufficient voice to say good-day with some firmness. As he got clear of the town two Clydesdales drawing a lorry trotted majestically past. The carter looked at him quizzically. Then John realized that he had a broad grin on his face and that he was bouncing up and down in his saddle. At once he sobered up. By the time he got back to the village the relief was still there but alongside it there still endured the terrible conviction that although physically he might be 'as sound as a bell' yet some sort of moral stain remained — a stain which must be apparent to anyone who cared to look closely.

That same autumn my father had his first major encounter with Miss Kerr, the infant teacher. She was an angular woman with red hair — dyed as Mrs Ramsay announced without fear of contradiction. She lived alone on the High Street with a couple of cats in a small house with a high walled garden, which the village boys scaled from time to time to rob her cherry tree in summer and later to pick the small, hard fruit from her two pear trees. She would lie in wait for them in her backroom but they were quick and nimble, usually big boys who had already left school, over whom she had no jurisdiction, although she felt she could recognize some of them in spite of the way their caps were pulled over their faces. But this autumn she caught a boy from the senior class — Frank Low whose father was a ploughman at Dalbog. Next day she came into the headmaster's room just after the morning hymn and denounced the boy, demanding that he be duly punished. My father's attitude was, as I have said, ambivalent; but he presumably knew that on this occasion he was caught by a system based on discipline through violent punishment and that, in a precise sense, his reputation with the pupils, with Miss Kerr and, through her, with the village was at stake. As Miss Kerr spoke Frank Low, summoned from his seat, stood in front of the class in his muddy boots and the big jacket in which he stored marbles, interesting pebbles, long shiny tapered pine-cones and sometimes a white mouse. He was rubbing his hands on the seams of his trousers, a process which was believed to take some of the sting out of the blows of the leather strap. Under interrogation he was mute. Told to hold out his hand he did so resolutely. The first stroke made him wince; two more made him thrust his swollen fingers between his knees to stifle the pain. 'The other hand,' said my father. Three more strokes. Back in his seat the boy pressed his hands against the cold iron legs of his desk; tears ran silently down his face. Miss Kerr walked triumphantly from the room. My father resumed the lesson. They were learning the physical features of Great Britain, beginning with the capes and promontories. But he had to make an effort to proceed for he was deeply shaken by conflicting sensations — a strange disgust, a revulsion against his own behaviour, and an equally disturbing sense of excitement that almost verged on pleasure — the same sensation as he had experienced as he lay and wept under the chastising hand of a cruelly loving mother. He would, he decided, have to make it up to the boy in some way — send him on an errand to the village store or praise his skill at carpentry.

This was not, however, his only encounter with Miss Kerr. At some level the incident with Frank Low may have contributed to the second one. In this case he felt in a more secure position for the issue was one of pedagogy. Miss Kerr's idea of teaching did not go much beyond rote-learning. So when he suggested that she took the class out on to the Muir to collect autumn leaves, identify and press them, then arrange them on stiff drawing paper, she bridled. She was, she said, not paid to be a nursemaid who took children out for walks. He left her classroom in a temper, calculating how much longer she had to serve, knowing that there was no possibility of persuading her to find another post and that no other headmaster within range of the village would accept her. After the mid-morning break he felt cooler and returning to the infant classroom intimated that he expected to see some improvement in her teaching methods — including the kind of nature study he had suggested — in default of which he would have to return a critical report to the Inspector at his next visit.

The matter came up at the next School Board meeting. It was the parish minister who raised it under any other business. He had heard. He informed the Board, that the headmaster had certain new-fangled ideas whereby members of his staff were to be required to leave the classroom and conduct the business of their profession — teaching — exposed to the public gaze. If this was what was being taught these days in training colleges things had come to a pretty pass. How could discipline be preserved if children were running wild on the Muir? What teacher could reasonably be required to perform her duties in front of half the village, subjected to the scorn of ignorant louts who would no doubt seize the opportunity to scoff? What children needed was discipline — that meant sitting at their desks, not talking, not fidgeting, learning the three R's. He had not heard that sticking dried leaves on paper had ever got any child very far in the world. The Chairman invited the headmaster to reply to the Rev. Tom Arnott's intervention. Mr Scott replied that in his view it was a matter of professional experience and that, in this area, he would, with respect, claim to have professional knowledge and to have studied some of the more recent and officially approved advances in pedagogy; these did not, to his certain knowledge, interfere with the aims of education to which the Rev Tom Arnott had referred and with which he was in total agreement: namely, the inculcation of the basic skills of reading, writing and the ability to count. But there was a further task, which was to lead children to take an interest in the world around them and to understand it better. Nature study of the kind he wished to introduce was part of that process. He would like to recall for the Board the first line of a well-known hymn which talked about 'all things bright and beautiful, all creatures great and small'. If they were appropriate to mention in an act of worship it seemed to him that they might be worthy of study. He also wished to remind the Board, again with respect, that in the last analysis he was responsible as a teacher under the

Scottish Education Act of 1872 not to the Board but to His Majesty's Inspectorate of Schools. At this point the Chairman declared that if there was no other business the meeting was closed.

The minutes in the bank agent's fine civil service hand gave no indication of the precise tone in which the Chairman brought the meeting to an end. When the members rose from the long table in the Memorial Hall and walked out into the Gothic vestibule the headmaster was aware of a space around him. Only the grocer crossed the invisible line of demarcation to say with a certain admiration: 'That was fine, Mr Scott. But I fear you went a wee bit far — just a wee bit far.' The Major and the parish minister walked off together in silent wrath. At the gate the Major stopped and waited. As the headmaster came abreast and raised his hat the Major stepped into his path. 'Young man,' he said, 'I do not like barrack-room lawyers. Never did like them. But I do know how to deal with them. Let me tell you — you got away with it this time. But I advise you not to try that game again.'

Through my head pass curious fragments of conversation I must have heard as a child. I would be sitting in my dressing gown at the dining-room table dipping a digestive in my hot milk when my father came back from a School Board meeting and told my mother of arguments, debates, resolutions in which people I knew in everyday life — like the village grocer and the parish minister, whose son was in my class at school — took on strange and somewhat frightening personalities which (so it seemed) were a threat to my parents and therefore to me. These half-intelligible exchanges were part of the mysterious life of work and the business of earning a living which I was excluded from (or perhaps protected from) right up to my adolescence; which may explain the pain and difficulty I experienced in learning to live in a real world — a world very different from that of books, lessons and irregular Latin verbs — where a mode of address at a committee meeting, a neutral-sounding minute, might spell demotion, loss of status, loss of employment even. Projecting into these memories of talk, half-heard and half-understood, later experiences in a great bureaucracy, I make sense of them, fabricate them into something coherent, something that will serve the strange process by which I string occasions, events, conversations, memories, into a narrative which, turning back a page to check a word, I find altogether surprising and unexpected.

My father told the story of his clash at the Board to Miss de Pass. Coffee and cakes had become a ritual on Saturday mornings. Usually the conversation opened with a report on the progress of his pupils or a discussion on the subject of reading matter: Why had he chosen *Treasure Island*, which was after all a children's book, when they were old enough to read something serious? Shaw, for instance. Or William Morris. *News from Nowhere*. He had to plead ignorance of Shaw or Morris — except for a couple of romantic poems with a medieval setting — and defended Stevenson on the grounds of the purity of his style and the range of his vocabulary. Miss de Pass shrugged and changed the subject to ask about school. How had he been getting along with the School Board for instance? He told her the story of the meeting, at which she laughed and said he had done well. Then she proceeded to an analysis of the Board and its constitution that left him bewildered and uncertain, although on reflection he had to concede that she made shrewd points, placing the parish minister, the Major and the big farmers in one faction with the Free Church minister and the grocer in another. The bank agent would sit on the fence, she argued; he needed everybody's money and therefore could not afford to offend anybody. That was why he had taken on the neutral job of secretary of the Board. 'And you? Where do you fit in?' she enquired. 'Are you by yourself? Or do you have allies? On the Board or outside — in the village?'

He replied that he felt the Free Church minister was more or less favourable to him and so was the grocer as an avowed Liberal; but he was a man of no education, opinionated, conceited, secure in his ignorance. That might be so, she countered, but on some issues he might be an ally. He had a virtual monopoly if you disregarded the other little store (run by an unmarried sister of Miss Kerr) so the conservatives couldn't take their custom elsewhere (that was the expression, wasn't it?) and he might see himself as the defender of Liberal causes in the Parish Council as well as on the School Board. Might even have ambitions to win election to the County Council. He could become important. 'So, Mr Scott, you should cultivate him a little. Don't be so fastidious. If everyone was nice and educated and read Racine — or if all our enemies were villains — politics would be a great deal easier.' Then she went on to ask who had instigated the parish minister's attack. He told her the story of nature study outdoors and of Miss Kerr's unreasonable objections, which were all the more unexplicable since — in a sense — she owed him a favour. Miss de Pass wanted to know what he meant by 'a favour'. He told her the story of the theft of the pears, about Miss Kerr's demand that Frank Low be punished and of how that punishment had been carried out. To his astonishment Miss de Pass got up and began to pace the room. When she stopped it was to rest her hand on the marble of the mantlepiece before turning to him with a white cold face to say: 'I shall tell you a story. In my country a man — a political prisoner awaiting trial — did not remove his hat when the governor visited the prison. The governor struck the man who did not reply. Next day the prisoner was flogged so mercilessly that he became insane.' The headmaster opened his mouth to interject something but she silenced him with a motion of the hand. 'Wait,' she said, 'my story is not finished. Next year a young woman who now lives in London — near King's Cross — joined the crowd presenting petitions to the Governor, drew a pistol and shot him. She did not resist arrest. Even the jury understood her motives. She was acquitted and escaped to England. You may think I come from a barbarous country. But that is what we think of corporal punishment.' She turned and walked from the room. My father sat for a moment then quietly rose, took his hat and coat and walked out of the house.

On his way back to Mrs Ramsay's he decided bleakly that his great fear had been realized — that one day he would for some reason be excluded from her company, that he would lose the key to this spot to which he felt drawn by a strange mixture of excitement, curiosity and intense pleasure which together amounted to a state which might, he felt, approximate to what people described as being in love: an idea he dismissed as too fantastic to contemplate. Yet now he was faced by the necessity, which he turned over in his mind that night and at various times during the following week, of writing to Miss de Pass a letter announcing that he regretted that he would no longer be able to continue to tutor David and Rachel, which he very much regretted although he fully understood her feelings. The problem was to find a formulation that might both express his hurt and anger and yet remain reasonably courteous so as to leave a possibility of re-entry. He cast and re-cast the text but by the following Saturday had not contrived to commit it to paper. Therefore just before ten o'clock he set out along a field path that brought him up the side of the villa. Why he should have chosen the field path rather than the usual road he might have been hard put to it to explain; but he was aware at the back of his mind that there was in his choice an element of subterfuge as if, by stealing up on the house, he might avoid something. What? A meeting with Miss de Pass? An attempt by Lienchen to refuse him entry? Some unequivocal signal from one or other child that he was unwelcome? Or perhaps it was merely so that he could withdraw unseen were he to lose his resolution, which was to ring the bell as if nothing had happened and risk being shown off the premises. To his surprise it was Miss de

Pass herself who opened the door and said with a smile that she hoped he would take coffee with her as usual after lessons were over.

When he knocked at the drawing-room and entered on hearing her Yes he found her standing in front of the fire in much the same pose as she had adopted a week before but this time her expression was no longer cold and forbidding. She was smoking a thin cheroot and poking a log back into the blaze with one foot. He stood uncertainly until she motioned him to a chair. When he sat down she blew out a puff of smoke and said, looking at him very openly: 'I wish to apologize. I had no right to behave as I did.' He was about to insist that there was no need for apologies but she motioned him to silence. 'I should not have attacked you as an individual,' she continued. 'I should have remembered that "the tradition of all the dead generations weighs like a nightmare on the brain of the living" and that you are the child of that nightmare. Yet I believe that it is possible for men and women to break out of that sleep of reason and to live freely, more rationally. You must not be angry. I am used to circles where people are very open with each other. I should like to think that we might achieve the same openness.'

It had been, he realized, as he walked back, taking the field path to avoid meeting any of the villagers in the street and having to stop and talk to them, some sort of turning-point in their relationship, a moment of communication which would place their conversation on a new footing. And so it proved. What he found himself responding to in this new situation was what had always drawn him back to the villa, the freedom and boldness of her thought, the coolness with which she pushed arguments into areas where he had half-hesitated to follow — a coolness balanced by the passion she showed when she spoke about politics — the vigour with which she made him confront the realities of his own life, compelling him to try to make sense of his childhood, of tenement life, of his mother's desperate energy and even of his father's drinking bouts. There was, he learned, a need in life to be principled — a state of mind which had nothing in common with the moralism of his upbringing with its appeal on the one hand to a cruel and punishing deity and on the other to mere gossip: 'What will people think? What will people say?' They were arguments which he absorbed with a sense of danger, for when he applied her precepts to his own case they led in simple logic to confrontation with the School Board of a violence that even in his daydreams caused him acute anxiety; yet he wished above all to please her and gain her approval. He had, she commented, been very principled over the question of nature study and one must understand that even the most apparently trivial issues could give rise to a principled stand. There were in all societies, even in a village like Slateford, occasions when the dominant powers could be challenged but one had to judge the moment and, as she had said before, one had to have allies. What, in this connection, had he been doing about the grocer?

All he could report was that he had been in touch with him in connection with the proposal for a Christmas treat for the village children in the village hall with a huge tree, donated by Major MacIllroy. They were on the organizing committee together and he would take the opportunity to talk about the School Board. To his surprise she was dismissive of the Christmas party saying that the big farmers would salve their consciences with a five pound note each as a contribution. But how did he intend to challenge the exploitation of child labour not only at the potato harvest but at harvest time and during the threshing of the grain or even when the sheep had to be driven to market? He listened and replied as best he could with excitement tinged with anxiety. What overcame his fears, what caused him to prolong these debates so long that on two occasions at least he returned to find Mrs Ramsay huffed and resentful and his dinner ostentatiously set by the fire to keep it warm, was excitement of another kind aroused by the way she talked — the play of her features, her smile and laugh (she laughed readily at some turn of phrase in his English that struck her as comical, or at a dialect word she had picked up in a village shop), her gestures — the way she shook her sleeve back on her arm with a faint click of bracelets, the way she sat down, the way she arranged her skirt when she crossed her legs, the movement of her hand to brush a hair away from her cheeks. There were moments when she showed him to the door and stood looking up into his face, for she was slightly shorter than he, when he was overwhelmingly tempted to move forward and do something — touch her face, kiss it perhaps — but was restrained by fear that if he did so he might incur her anger and find his entrance for ever barred.

Over and above such fascinations there was the sheer interest with which he learned of the experience of life which had formed her. Out of occasional glimpses, casual references, he began to erect a biography that spanned certainly Vienna, probably Berlin, undoubtedly Paris and other locations between which — or so it seemed — she moved effortlessly and at will: a mode of travelling he contrasted mentally with his own struggle across Paris from the Gare du Nord to the Gare d'Austerlitz in a cab with his tin trunk and Gladstone bag. He was in all ways immensely curious about her with the curiosity of a small boy faced by an unimaginable treasure of half-guessed secrets and unspoken reticences. There were names that cropped up in her talk with or without explanation: Rosa, with whom she corresponded, who was Polish and a revolutionary; Paul, who was the father of David and Rachel; someone who she referred to with a laugh as Prince Myshkin — had he read Dostoevsky's *Idiot* — no? — then he must, but she only had it in the original — then he would understand what she meant: a man with a beard and a curiously naïve face who had stopped her in the street (she was attending some conference in Vienna) and asked her for the loan of fifty schillings. His name? Bukharin, a holy fool like Prince Myshkin but a good economist. And someone called Boris, whom she mentioned once, then stopped so that a silence followed which she broke by lighting one of her long, slim cheroots. And beyond these secrets of her mind and of her history, there were the secrets of her body to guess at which he had for reference only images he felt obliged to censor: images of the women standing round Tante Marie, surprisingly fat with hips and breasts of an unexpected variety of shapes and sizes. But the shape of hers he could not guess through her loose blouses although he was aware of and fascinated by its soft gentle movement when she bent and stretched in her chair.

Just before Christmas he arrived one Saturday to find the children preparing candles in a branched candlestick. It surprised him, for he had not expected her to set much store by Christmas — or indeed for any of the festivals of the Church. After the lesson they sat by the fire, which was pungent with resin from the pine logs and fat cones from the garden. He felt freer now and could ask a question: What were the candles for? She looked at him with a certain surprise 'For Hanukkah, of course.' At this bewilderment she burst out laughing. 'A festival of light,' she explained, 'to celebrate the victory of the Maccabees over the Romans.' He knew about the rising of the Maccabees against imperial Rome from his reading of history but why the celebration? Seeing his bewilderment continue, she stopped laughing and said with sudden seriousness: 'Don't you know we are Jewish? That you are a goy, that if I were an orthodox Jewess instead of a woman over whom her father said a prayer for the dead I could not sit with you or eat with you or let you teach the children. 'A goy?' he asked. 'A non-Jew,' she explained, 'not one of the children of Israel, not one of the chosen — though I wonder sometimes what we were chosen for — not circumcised. You must know what a Jew is. Don't you read the Old Testament in church?'

Place these events in provincial Scotland before the First World War and you will understand his ignorance. Twenty years later in the same province it was possible for me and my class-mates, both boys and girls, to leave school with only the vaguest idea about the Jews, who were a chosen race to be equated somehow with the Presbyterian Scots in that they displayed, to judge by the Old Testament, the same virtues of obedience to a divine power, to hard work and the observance of the laws of God, the same combination of thrift and combativeness. They had also, more puzzlingly, but it was not something that was ever elucidated either in church, in Bible class or in scripture lessons in school, an intense interest in foreskins which they appeared to collect from the Philistine dead. They also produced some splendid poetry which was in some indelible way part of our own culture. They were also responsible for that strict observance of the Sabbath which prevented us from swimming on Sunday or skating in winter when the ponds froze over or from playing golf on the town links. And they had been rather nasty to Jesus but he was, in my eyes at least, a less impressive figure than some of the Old Testament heroes like David or Joshua, who, so our English teacher — unmarried because as the whole town knew, her fiancé was killed in Flanders — reminded us, was a military figure comparable perhaps only to Earl Haig, commander of the British forces in the long battles of the Passchendaele and the Somme. But the community in which we grew up contained, so far as we knew, no Jews, who occurred only in the Bible or in Shakespeare. At university we would meet young men and women whom we might with some puzzlement identify as Jews. With them we found ourselves demonstrating against the advance of Fascism in Germany and the way in which it threatened to spill over into Britain. But what a Jew was, except someone with an ancient culture, persecuted by a great modern tyranny that threatened many others besides the Jews, we would have been at a loss to say. There was Palestine where Jews and Arabs were involved in struggles which, in obscure and complicated ways, affected British colonial interests; there was something called Zionism which raised political problems but — so the line ran (a word I use with specific reference to the political line of the Communist Party or at least the Young Communist League) — Zionism would soon be overcome in a movement of unity which would weld

Jew and Arab into a single proletariat that would rise up to overcome Fascism and imperialism. It was a vision which obliterated the Jew of the Old Testament and made Shylock relevant only in so far as the malevolence of Portia's glib tongue prefigured the obscenities of a Nazi-like Streicher, in which pornography, sexual envy and racism were mingled. So how should John Scott have known what it meant to be a goy, what the high holidays were or guess at the childish delights of Hanukkah?

How much did she tell him? I imagine she turned away some of his questions on religion and explained that for her they were less important than political and social ones. Yet during these months, as their friendship grew, he must have learned something about the Jewish communities in the Pale of the Settlement and the life of the shtetl. Perhaps she told him stories about the Wunder-rabbis with their curious blend of piety and humour. She would tell, from her own experience, what it was like to be addressed by a customs official using the grammatical forms reserved for inferiors, to be called a *Zhid* or to suffer, as a bright boy or girl exclusion from university or college because of the *numerus clausus*. But anti-Semitism, she no doubt explained to him, she saw — to take the Dreyfus case as an example — as the expression of deeply reactionary trends in society where the poor and exploited projected on to the Jewish employer the cumulative faults of the capitalist class and the ruling class saw in the Jews the fomentors of revolution; so the Jews, as centre and focus of some vast world conspiracy were at one and the same time exploiters and revolutionaries: either way the scapegoats who proudly marked themselves, defined themselves as a target, by dress and language, by dietary and other religious laws. At this point, as often happened in their talks, he began to feel out of his depth so that he could not even formulate the questions that might have brought explanations. But such moments were less troubling than others when he felt excluded, jealous of those names without faces who lived in her talk and her memories with some of whom she had a relationship defined by the words 'very fond'. At the back of his mind, too, colouring his pleasure in her company, so that it was shot through with sudden shafts of sadness, was the recognition that their relationship was by its nature transient, that any day she might take off — like the swallows and swifts — and disappear, constrained by a logic to which he was not privy, answering a summons that came from places and persons beyond his ken. What he did realize was that — if by a miracle he were to be admitted to those circles of which she spoke and among which she had lived — he would have to venture greatly and change greatly. He wondered whether he was capable of such a metamorphosis. At the same time he was aware of what he might have described had he known the concept, as a heightened sensibility: when he was with her he seemed to be more aware of the taste of a cake, the smell of a burning pine-log, the perfume of her warm body, the colour of a scarf she wore, the feel of the path under his feet as he hurried across the fields, the chill of a winter shower, the crispness of untrodden frozen snow, the deer on the hillside above the village searching for fodder in the fields.

Yet was there, he reflected sometimes, as he walked back to the village, anything to justify his agitation? The question revolved in his mind for days. There was, he felt, a gulf of improbability set between himself and Elizavyeta — he had begun to think of her by her first name — that discouraged fantasies about some sort of relationship which he found it hard to define; but which did not prevent the continuance of just such fantasies that produced and fed on a kind of longing both physical and mental, a hunger and a desire which had only one object, one impossible consummation. When he reflected soberly, he could not imagine her wishing to become the wife of a village schoolmaster and, although he knew from literature that there could be liaisons between men and women who were not married, he found it difficult to imagine himself involved in such a situation. With May he had known — for a time at least — where he stood. There was a basis there for a commonsense sober arrangement which would liberate her from her mother's tyranny and provide her with secure status as a married woman and, perhaps, as a mother, wife of a headmaster who might be promoted to a school in Dundee or further afield still, becoming in the course of time one of His Majesty's Inspectors of Schools. Such things were not unknown. But though they still saw each other on Sundays his exchanges with May were now brief. Mrs Mitchell for her part was barely civil and only the miller appeared unchanged, though what he truly thought and felt might well be concealed by his beard. Phemy was mischievous, feigning surprise when she met him in the village street or at the church door over the fact that she hadn't seen him at the mill for a while and relaying reports about Jim's progress as a mechanic. All of which was trivial and irrelevant compared to what he experienced each Saturday morning as he responded to a freedom and boldness of thought such as he had seldom met and had indeed not thought possible in a woman.

Some of his new awareness and openness to experience he took with him to the Christmas treat in the village hall, where the tree rose twenty feet into the air, securely anchored in the middle of the floor, sombre yet graceful, its lower branches hung about with tinsel and little candles while from a ladder Willie Hamilton precariously stretched his arm to fix a silver star to the highest tip. At the door a couple of girls handed him a paper bag that held a couple of sandwiches, a currant slice, a cake and a handful of almonds and raisins. Slowly the hall began to fill and the platform party climbed up into their places. His seat as headmaster was between the Free Church minister and the grocer. There was an empty place for Major MacIllroy, who was suddenly there in the hall with his sister at his side. A hush fell as he escorted her to a place on the platform and then, resplendent in the dubious tartan of his clan, his jabots and silver-chased sporran, the skean dubh in his stocking set with a dark cairngorm stone, called for silence in a voice that, in its day, had echoed over barrack-squares in Bangalore, Aden and Fort George. In the hush that followed he called on the Reverend Tom Arnott to offer up a short prayer — there was an almost imperceptible stress on the word 'short'. The minister rose and in the nasal drone of his calling invoked the blessing of the Almighty on those assembled there, on Major MacIllroy in particular, and through the mediation of the Most Holy called down blessings on the village and its benefactors. The Major heard him out patiently then rose to announce that carols would be sung and that he expected to be able to hear them properly sung, beginning with Once in royal David's city. John Scott, rising to his feet, could not see but could guess how May took her place at the piano and with a brief introductory flourish led them in the singing. For the first time he was conscious of the irony of this celebration of a king who was, after all, the David of the star which Rachel sometimes wore on her necklace but who had been appropriated by Christianity.

Then came the time for the distribution of presents for which he had to go down to a long table on the floor of the hall and with Miss Troup and Miss Kerr see to it that each child got something as he called out the names from the school register. Willie Hamilton drew the gifts from a couple of coarse jute sacks: a tin toy, a trumpet, a toy soldier, a rag doll, and for the older children a knife perhaps or a handkerchief, a skipping rope or a top, received with joy or disappointment. Spruced up for the occasion by their parents or an elder sister, the children wore their Sunday best or whatever approximated to it. Once they had been to the table they turned, usually without more than a mumbled thanks and retreated to examine what luck had brought them and then trade off unwanted objects in dark corners of the hall: a couple of coloured marbles for a tin horse or a sheet of transfers. At the end, there was a pause filled by the wailing of a small boy brought to the table by his brother who protested: 'Please sir, he hasnae got naething. He hasnae got naething.' Miss Troup turned the sacks out till a wooden whistle fell on the floor. The wailing died instantly. The headmaster looked at Miss Troup who smiled. As they piled the empty sacks away under the table their hands touched and their eyes met. He felt suddenly as if he had not seen her properly before — not noticed, for instance, the short dark curls at the back of her neck where her hair was swept up to the top of her head. Or the white line of her rather small teeth. 'What's next?' he asked less because he wanted to know than to cover a moment's embarrassment. 'Tea,' she replied and to his astonishment wanted to know what he had got in his paper-bag. Her question took him aback. It was the first time that they had talked about anything informally other than the business of the school or, at most, the weather. He was aware of her Highland accent, which the children found slightly comical so that more than once he had to rebuke them for a snigger when she announced the morning hymn. He had opened his 'poke' when Willie Hamilton came up and said 'Miss, you're needed for the games'. With a quick backward glance she was off to lead the company, partnered by the Major himself, in the Grand Old Duke of York and Here We Go Lubin Loo, after which dances succeeded to games and she was the leading figure in the Lancers, the Eightsome Reel, Strip the Willow — not to mention the Dashing White Sergeant in which the headmaster was reluctantly involved, for dancing was not one of his accomplishments, with Mrs Ramsay on one arm and the grocer's wife on the other.

Inevitably as the dance progressed and the trios advanced and retired, passed through and met yet another three dancers, he found himself facing in turn May and Phemy and Miss Troup, who he wished were on his arm and not on that of a young farmer from Stracathro way to whom she 'set' in the reel and then swung on his arm with a flush running up into her dark hair. Then at last tea did come; bags were produced or retrieved and the hall was filled with groups as people drew chairs together or lined up before the great tea urns. Sugar sweets in pink or white with mottoes on them like Kiss me or I love you were exhibited, deprecated, exchanged or thrust on embarrassed girls and shy youths with their hair slicked down with water. Afterwards there were waltzes and more reels for which Willie Hamilton played his violin with a style that linked him to the musicians at the barn–dances he had gone to as a young soldier back on leave. John Scott was unfamiliar with the intricacies of the reels and awkward when his turn came to step into the middle of the circle and set to each woman in turn, so he welcomed the excuse to talk to the Rev. James Murdoch and his wife, a lady with a frighteningly severe air and an imposing bust but who was pleased to praise the tree and even to comment favourably on the behaviour of the children. It was noticeable that none of her own children were there although they had come back from their boarding-school for the Christmas holidays. 'We'll have to get Mr Scott married,' said the minister, 'the school–house will be ready in the spring.' His wife agreed and commented that it was a miserable life, a bachelor's.

As soon as he might the headmaster excused himself and started to walk over to the corner where the grocer, looking more like Lloyd George than ever, was sharing a joke with a couple of young farmers. John Scott could guess the kind of joke it was from the guffaws that went up and the quick look over his shoulder the grocer gave before he drove home the point. He himself knew only a few mild jokes which, so his brother always said, he told in such a way that the point was lost. He was still a couple of yards away from the group when Miss MacIllroy intercepted him. 'Good evening, headmaster,' she said, adjusting the Celtic brooch that held her tartan sash at the shoulder, 'I hope you are enjoying yourself. Tell me,' she went on with an impetus that allowed of no interruption on his part, 'I believe that you tutor the children who live with that foreign lady, Miss de Pass. We invited her to the Burnfoot once, just after she arrived. She seemed quite ladylike really and very polite. But with some very dangerous ideas. What is she really? I know her name sounds French but I don't believe it. I told the Major the other day that I do believe the woman is a Jewess. That would explain everything. She never goes to church. Never mixes with people. Very odd. Living alone with that foreign housekeeper of hers and these children who do not appear to have any formal education. Do you know whose they are, Mr Scott? But of course you must, you are their teacher.' It was instinct rather than any clear understanding of why he did it that made John Scott lie. He really did not know what nationality Miss de Pass was. He believed that the children's parents were relations of hers. They came from Switzerland, or so he understood, but they seemed to have moved about a good deal. They were bright children and good pupils. And what language did the lady speak, might she ask? French presumably. Miss MacIllroy understood he had spent some time in France, in Perpignan was it not? (He wondered how she had learned, what chain of gossip had led from Mrs Ramsay to the Major's sister.) She herself had been to the Riviera several times — to Nice to be precise — and had managed perfectly well without French but she supposed one had to learn it — although what good a knowledge of French did if you were teaching ploughboys and servant girls, she did not know. Suddenly she switched the conversation. 'I believe you have some very advanced ideas about education, Mr Scott. I always think that if a child leaves school able to read, able to write a legible hand and able to add pennies and ha'pennies that is all one can hope for or indeed should strive for. By the way, we need a good dependable girl to look after the Major's nephews and nieces when they come to visit us at Easter. Can you recommend anyone? Or would that be against your principles?' He assured her that it would not and pointed out a girl who was solicitously helping the small ones on with their coats. Miss MacIllroy made an inclination of the head that could perhaps have been interpreted as thanks and walked off to examine the girl more closely and to interrogate her.

The headmaster himself looked round the emptying hall to see if he could catch sight of Miss Troup. What motivated him in his search was a strange excitement, which his brother would no doubt have described as a state of randiness. He was just in time to see her walk off, high-spirited and vivacious and rather red in the face with the young farmer from Stracathro. He put on his hat and coat, said goodnight to the caretaker of the hall and to Willie Hamilton, who was busy stacking chairs and collecting the debris of the party, stopping every so often to check that the five shillings the Major had given him was still there in his pocket and regretting that the bar in the Central Hotel in Church Street would by now be shut — although maybe he could sneak in and persuade the proprietor, a drinking friend of his, to let him have a couple of drams. Outside the moon was white and frozen. In the east Orion was climbing the sky. Above the hills, as the headmaster walked homewards, crunching the ice in the puddles, the Northern Lights flared fitfully across the sky in iridescent sheets. Mrs Ramsay was there before him. Had he seen Miss Troup and the way she was carrying on with young Adams of Stracathro she asked, fair setting her cap at him? 'Mind you she's a bonny lass and a famous dancer. But there's more to coortin' than dancing as she'll soon find out — if I know young Adams.' She laughed suddenly then became serious again. 'Well, I suppose it's bedtime.' For the first time her lodger, as he watched her go up the stairs, was aware that she was a handsome woman and still in her prime of life.

After Hanukkah, David and Rachel left for London. His fears that Miss de Pass might accompany them she dispelled saying she would only go as far as Perth and there put them on the sleeper; a friend would meet them in London. What were his plans for the holidays? He supposed he would be going to his mother's. She understood she said that there was a custom in Scotland of celebrating the New Year with a ceremony that had a strange name. 'First footing,' he said and explained how the gift of a lump of coal presented on the threshold of the house ensured prosperity for the coming year. She laughed. 'We have the concept of bread and salt.' In fact there was one concept and one word — bread-salt as it were — and she spoke the word then asked him to repeat it; but he could not get his tongue round the liquid 'l' in which it ended. Would he then be back for the New Year and if so would he come to wish her prosperity? He said Yes at once although he could imagine the tearful scene his mother would make if he did not spend Hogmanay with her. He could hear her plaint: how one son was across the seas and heaven knew when he might come back, another in London and the one who was still in Scotland could not be bothered with 'a puir body' — couldn't even stay 'to see the Auld Year oot.'

Which was how it was, except that his brother Tom actually came up from London, walking cockily up the street from the station with a smart trilby, kid gloves and spats over his shoes. He smoked his cigarette in an ivory holder, spent his evenings roller skating or at the Bioscope Cinema, watching what his mother called trash or — as she could tell from her experience with his father — drinking into the bargain. 'O, mither,' he said, parodying his Scottish accent, 'what's wrang wi' a dram noo and then.' Then to annoy them he switched to Cockney and sang a song about how 'my old man said follow the van'. A great song, he said, they should hear Marie Lloyd sing it. His mother listened sourly to his chat about the great city and life in the south. She had no great opinion of 'they English' and hoped he wasn't going to bring some English girl home as his fiancée, talking that silly way they had and no doubt going to pubs and suchlike places. Oh, yes, she had heard — she knew more than he thought — women did go in pubs in England but no self-respecting woman in Scotland would cross the doorway into a public bar. 'Toodleloo, mum,' said the prodigal and, knocking his hat on to his head at an angle, was away out of the front door and down the tenement stairs.

John himself was as attentive as he could bring himself to be. He accompanied his mother to the family grave in a village churchyard under the Ochil Hills. They travelled out by horse-drawn tram. The grave was reasonably well-kept; there was plenty of space, his mother pointed out, for her name on the stone, when the time came, which she hoped might not be long now, for there was little left to live for. She picked up a few withered flowers left from some summertime visit and ran her hand over the polished red granite of the headstone. With a certain astonished embarrassment John heard her say his father's name in tones of genuine grief. He wondered whether he had not perhaps misunderstood or misread the relationship between his parents and reflected that there must have been a time when they, too, felt a sudden excitement, catching sight of each other in church or at a fair, and had walked hand in hand along the side of the Forth or looked out from the castle ramparts to the Highland hills. When he and his mother got home their feet were frozen from a ride that was slow because the horse's hooves kept slithering on the thin layer of black frost on the road. He had meant to tell her that day that he would not be staying to see the New Year in; but he did not have the heart to do so. In the end he had the courage to break the news only a couple of days before his departure. His sister was furious with him. It was all right for him to go off but she had to stay and listen to her mother weeping and wailing; in any case was it so much to ask that he should give an old body that little bit of pleasure. What would happen if she decided to go gallivanting off and leave her mother all by herself? But she knew she would never be able to get away — not till her mother was dead and buried although God forbid that should come so soon. She would end up an old maid looking after a poor old body that could do nothing but sit by the fire and whine. Oh, it was a fine thing to be a man and just do what you liked but why should a young woman like herself sacrifice her life and little thanks for it?

His sister's words and his mother's lament that her sons were abandoning her on the very night they should all be together accompanied him on his way to the station. There was a thin powdering of snow on the road; hard frost glistened on the rails of the sidings and on the sleepers between the rails. A weak afternoon sun touched the window by which he found a seat but when he leant into his corner he could feel the cold seep through the wood and metal of the carriage wall. There were three other men in the compartment playing some card-game and managing the pack with astonishing and practised dexterity. They invited him to join in but he remembered his brother's talk about cardsharpers and their tricks which he, ever knowing, claimed he could detect and indeed would proceed to demonstrate, inviting his listeners to 'spot the lady' as he flicked the cards just as these men did now. They took John's refusal goodnaturedly and went on with their game, during the course of which money changed hands at a considerable speed. One of them produced a flask of whiskey and passed it to his fellow players. 'A drap o' the auld kirk,' he said to John, extending the flask with a gesture which was wholly ironical and expected refusal. John shook his head. The man laughed and said something about not knowing what was good for you and being stuck up. The train had climbed up into the hills and was panting towards the watershed where the land would level out before falling away towards Perth and Carse of Gowrie. Beside a lonely loch in the moorland bonfires glowed and flickered in the afternoon twilight; the figures of skaters and curlers were briefly silhouetted against the flames. 'A great game that,' said one of the card-players. 'Aye,' another concurred, 'the roaring game.' The game went on with a soft clink of coins and a laugh or a curse. The snow was deeper here; pale expanses of hillside rose to the darkening sky. Outside Perth there was a long wait at a signal. 'Well, we've been lucky this far,' said one of the men. 'My brother's on the railway. Highland Line. They've had the snowploughs out north of Perth.'

John in his corner was turning over in his mind a stratagem, a course of action, that would enable him to keep his promise and first foot Miss de Pass. It was an enterprise which, now as he looked out at the pale landscape, took form in fantasies which he allowed to drift through his mind, shaping and reshaping them with a mixture of excitement and apprehension. But they were curiously vague at crucial points and he broke off in uncertainty, for he had no sense of how he might bring them to a conclusion or indeed what conclusions were possible. In any case more practical considerations kept intruding and incorporating themselves in his daydreams: they included the fact that Mrs Ramsay would be expecting him off the last train at eight o'clock, would no doubt have his supper ready and would be extremely surprised, not to say suspicious, if he let himself in in the small hours — an entrance which she was sure to register. He turned over in his mind possible excuses but none of them had a convincing ring — although the mention of snowploughs and blocked lines held some promise. At Perth station two of the card-players got out leaving the third man, drunk and half-asleep and slumped in a corner of the carriage. John too left the train to buy himself a cup of tea and a hot pie at the station buffet. The train, he learned, was half-an-hour late and there was trouble with the signals further up the track because of icing and snow drifting on to the line.

More than an hour later the train drew up at the wayside junction where he had changed trains on his way to take up his appointment in Slateford. The man in the corner got out too, feeling in his pockets and swearing to himself when he found them empty. The station porter was gloomy and cast doubts on the possibility of getting much further that night. The weather had played the devil with the timetables. John walked into the little waiting-room where a huge fire was volcanic with sparks that sent great tongues of flame chasing them up the chimney. The card-player hawked noisily and spat into the flames and wondered whether John didn't have a drop of something to keep out the cold. Receiving a negative reply he slumped down beside a group of dejected travellers who lined the benches round the walls and exchanged gloomy prognoses. But in spite of them the train did at last emerge slowly out of the darkness in which the glow from its fire-box and the occasional bright cinder thrown up from the funnel were like some kind of eruption. It did not leave at once, however, but waited — for a connection from the north, said the porter, which eventually drew up at the platform with a silver coating of frost on the engine and carriages, hissed and belched steam for a few minutes, and then slowly got under way to London.

At last John's train moved off. The carriages were glacial; John found himself regretting the warm fug set up by the card-players who no doubt were cosy somewhere, spending their winnings, eating, drinking and gambling the old year out. There was little he could do, however, except wrap his coat tightly round himself and drum his feet on the carriage floor to keep the circulation going.

When they arrived at Slateford — which would be very late if indeed they arrived at all — he would decide on a plan in which the state of the railways and the chaos the winter weather had wrought with the timetables would play a part; but the details of his story were unclear to him: all he was sure of was his determination to reach the villa at midnight or just after. With extreme slowness the train made its way along the wide strath, passing beneath the hills and the Iron Age fort where he had found Elizavyeta. It was no doubt filled deep with drifted snow and protected by a glacis of ice. In a long gentle curve the line took them into the market town from which the branch line ran to Slateford. The station clock said ten. A porter with a scarf wrapped round his neck and a red dripping nose announced that there was no question of the train pro-ceeding to Slateford that night. What do I do then? John asked. The porter ignored his rhetorical question, but he took heart at the thought that after all it was only six miles to the village and that his only luggage was his Gladstone bag. He would try walking. If the road was passable it should not take him more than a couple of hours at the most. Once outside the station John looked up at the sky which was no longer overcast although not as bright as on the night of the village party. Orion was higher in the sky but there were no Northern Lights, no Merry Dancers.

As he got clear of the town and set his face to the hill, the snow was compacted under foot; even out in the country it was trodden down by horses' hooves and the iron-rimmed wheels of the farm-carts. A fresh fall had merely laid a thin cushion of soft snow on the tracks so that he had little difficulty in walking. His circulation began to revive with the effort although his nose and ears were sharp with cold. An hour later he was following the geometrically precise line of the road as it skirted a field which still preserved the configuration of a Roman camp; he could see the dark outline of the steading set in a corner of the ramparts and the light of an oil-lamp in the kitchen window. He felt a longing for the kind of warmth that must surround it. Then he was walking by a stream which he could hear running with a tinkling sound under the frozen snow and among the icy stones. Soon he would be more than halfway there and would see in front of him the dark compact mass of pines that stretched for a mile in front of the village. From somewhere behind he thought he heard a voice encouraging a horse, the creak of a badly oiled wheel and the jingle of harness. Turning he could see, some four hundred yards down the road, the faint flicker of an oil-lamp on a trap or gig. Slowly it drew up with him with the horse's hooves making a dull thud on the snow. Coming alongside it halted. 'Jump up, headmaster,' said the driver, as the horse shifted its feet to get a firm grip in the snow. It was young Adams from Stracathro who had escorted Miss Troup from the party. 'Just in time for first footing then?' John Scott said he thought he'd maybe just go straight to bed. He'd had a terrible journey. Conversation died. Under the cover of the horse-blanket spread over his knees John felt warmer. The farmer shook his reins every now and again and clicked his tongue; the hooves beat evenly on the surface of the snow with a drumming sound; the wheel creaked with a regular rhythm. The farmer cursed the noise and then fell silent again.

Where the woods began they could see straight up the road to the village. Occasionally there was a rustle of branches and the patter of snow falling on to the pine-needles beneath the trees as a capercailzie or woodcock stirred in the tree-tops. Just beyond the village hall the farmer pulled in his horse and said he'd have to drop his passenger here because he was off for a dram with Keillor of Bogside. Then with a ritual 'Guid New Year' he drove off. The village clock showed half-past eleven. John felt a sense of relief. He had arrived in time. The farmer lived outside the village. No doubt he would tell Mr Keillor that he had found the dominie walking along the road in the snow but with luck the story would stay on the fringes of village society and not get to Mrs Ramsay's ears. There was always Miss Troup, of course, but she was not due back from holiday for a couple of days at least. Even though she was the link between the village and young Adams he had a feeling that she would not necessarily wish to admit that she had heard the story from that source.

He had then only half-an-hour to wait till he could knock on the door of the villa and make his ritual offering: the small lump of gleaming coal on which one could see the delicate tracery of a fossil fern, now lying in his Gladstone bag, wrapped in thin paper. His mother had found him picking through the lumps in the coalshed at the back of the tenement block and had begun to interrogate him but he put her off by saying that he needed a piece for a lesson on coal formations and fossils. She said she thought there were maybe more useful things the bairns could learn but did not pursue the subject. She watched sourly as he split the coal with a hammer to reveal the fossil at its heart. The sight had caused him to cry out with pleasure. He walked up the deserted street where the glass of the street lamps was veiled by a layer of frozen snow. Turning off Church Street he took the path through the fields; his feet sank at every step for no-one had passed this way since the first heavy fall. He was, he reflected, leaving a very clear trace but it was too late to turn back and, in any case, there might well be a fresh fall before day-break. When he reached the wooden fence that ran alongside the tanglewood of wild raspberries he looked up and saw the light burning in the study window. It threw an oblong path of yellow on to the unbroken snow. In the drive up through the pines the snow had been shovelled in mounds to either side. He made not for the front door but for the summer hut, the rustic shelter where in summer Miss de Pass sat and read among the trees on the hillock that looked out towards the West Water and the road leading to the fort. The snow had sifted through the cracks in the walls of the hut but the seat was clear and there was an illusory feeling of warmth. He sat down and began his wait. Southwards Orion was now almost at its zenith; the Plough dangled brightly to the north. An immense silence lay over the countryside except when some tree creaked as the frost bit into its branches. He had taken the coal and salt from his Gladstone bag and laid them on the wooden seat beside him. He ran his cold fingers over the smooth face of the coal and fancied he could just detect the pattern of the fossil fern.

After a time the clock in the village hall rang quarter to the hour; perhaps if he could have read the time might have passed more quickly but the white glimmer of light from the snow was merely deceptive and there was no moon. He felt the night air penetrate through his coat and clothes till it found his skin. He rubbed his hands together and flapped his arms against his sides. Stamping his feet in the snow and thrusting his hands into his arm-pits he tried to revive the circulation. He was too cold to think about the story he would concoct for Mrs Ramsay or for Miss Troup should she ever raise the subject of New Year's Eve; in a curious way it hardly seemed to matter. When midnight rang out at last in the still air, he slipped the coal into a coat pocket, picked up his Gladstone bag and walked up to the front door. If his fingers hesitated on the bell it was as much as anything else because he had difficulty in finding it. When he pressed the button he could hear a faint tinkle somewhere deep inside the house. There was a long pause and then what appeared to be a lighted candle moved through the back of the hall. He could see a brighter light as the study door opened. In the interval he imagined a conversation between Lienchen and Elizavyeta, a brief consultation in whatever language it was that Lienchen habitually spoke. Was it an exchange of fears? or had she remembered his promise to fulfil the ritual? At last a light came on in the hall and a shadow fell on the glass of the door. Before it opened Elizavyeta's voice asked very calmly: 'Who is there?' 'Me,' he replied whereupon the door opened and with a laugh she said: 'Mr Scott. Come in.' But on the threshold he laid down his bag and from his pocket produced the nugget of coal and held it out to her. 'I've come first footing — as I promised,' and added the ritual formula: 'A guid New Year tae ane and a' '. 'S novim godom,' she replied and accepted the offering; the Russian phrase he experienced as a welcoming sound. From the hall he could already feel the heat of the house flow round him. He laid his bag on the hall table with its large brass oriental gong, hung his coat and hat on the hat-stand and followed her into the drawingroom where she was on her knees poking the embers and adding fresh logs which, as they fell into the hearth, sent showers of sparks up the chimney.

'What should one do to welcome someone who comes first footing?' she asked, poking the logs with her foot with a gesture he knew well. 'Offer him something to drink, I imagine. A dram, as you might say.' From a corner cupboard she took a tray with two small glasses and a bottle. 'Vodka,' she said. 'I have no whiskey. I don't like it, I'm afraid.' 'I don't like it that much either,' he confessed. 'But this is good vodka from Poland,' she went on and held the bottle up to the light to show the feathery herb that lay in the spirits. 'It gives it a special taste.' She filled the glasses. 'You must drink it like this,' she instructed him and, touching his glass with a quick 'Good health', tossed off her glass. He tried to imitate her but the spirits caught at the back of his throat and had him coughing and embarrassed. She took his glass from him. 'It takes practice,' she said. Their fingers touched on the stem of the glass. 'But you're frozen. Sit down. Get warm.' There was a silence between them for a moment. Then she suddenly said: 'You mustn't think I had forgotten that you had promised to come. But Lienchen was afraid. She comes from a society where the police like to knock at midnight. I know her fears. I have been afraid myself. So I had to reassure her.' She took the poker and made a space under the logs — a red tunnel in which the flame grew and licked up round the odourous bark. Then she said: 'Tell me about your holiday.'

What he talked about was his family — about the visit to his father's grave and his sister's bitterness but more than anything else about his brother and the strange life he led in London and the certainty, the knowingness with which he talked about girls, about cardsharpers, about the tricks and stratagems of life, drawing on a store of experience which made him feel naïve and innocent. But he himself had been abroad, she objected, was how old? nearly thirty? And what, she wanted to know, was so surprising about a certain knowledge of the world and what went on in it? Besides presumably even in Slateford things went on? He laughed and said Yes, there was the woman in the cottage just down from the school with three or four children and no obvious husband. There was the ex-barmaid from the hotel who lived in the High Street just opposite Miss Kerr — and much to her disgust — in a house that belonged to a lawyer in Dundee. There was the son of the man who kept the stables, and had acquired the motor-car; he cycled all round the countryside in search of girls and was rumoured to have one on most of the big farms and, what was more, was believed to have found his way into the bedroom of the daughter of a minister up one of the glens by climbing up a ladder when her parents slept. How did he know all this? she asked laughing, and was it very different from his brother's knowledge of London life? What was his source? Mrs Ramsay? He admitted it was and she burst out laughing — so he wasn't quite the innocent he made himself out to be. Her next question he found so astonishing that he sat for a moment almost as if he had not heard it holding his hands out to the fire to shield his face, as if suddenly the heat had become intolerable. Her question was short and to the point: 'What about your experience of life?' He returned his hands to his lap and attempted to deflect her question. 'What experience?' 'You know very well what I meant. Your experience with women. You must have had some. Or were there no nice girls in France?' He was silent as if struck dumb for how could he tell her about Tante Marie? But she did not relent in her interrogation, pointing out that he knew — must know that she had some experience of men, after all she had been married — and that while marriage might be socially necessary in some circumstances — which were mostly to do, incidentally, with the ownership of property and similar matters — she saw nothing wrong in sexual relationships between people who liked and had a regard for one another, people one was fond of. For a moment he was silent reflecting on the phrase 'to be fond of someone' and finding his jealousies and suspicions around her trip to Vienna substantiated; but he could not maintain his silence for ever and found himself saying: 'Very little.' She looked at him quizzically and repeated: 'Very little — experience, you mean?' He found himself explaining the constraints of his upbringing and of the society into which he had been born. She listened with attention, nodding agreement from time to time. But when he had finished she had an objection; we were not always and for ever the prisoners of our social or family background — otherwise there would be no possibility of breaking through the chains of class, no possibility of rejecting the intolerable constraint of religion. Then, as if in answer to his openness, she began for the first time to tell something of her own childhood and adolescence in the oppressive closeness of a small textile manufacturing town in Eastern Poland, the claustrophobia of the ghetto and the intense, narrow religious life from which she was a woman excluded, being allowed to look down from the women's gallery to the floor of the synagogue where the men talked and gossiped as they waited for the great scrolls of the law to be produced from their tabernacle. She spoke with anger and resentment but to him there was something about the life she described, something immensely exciting and exotic, strange and legendary with its great festivals of Purim and Tabernacles, the joy of Pesach, the solemnity of Yom Kippur, the chanting of the wandering Talmud scholars who came to the house to study with her father, Reb Itzak, the stories of the wonder-rabbis and the rituals of daily life. She sensed his reaction and countered it with an attack on religious orthodoxy, on narrow-mindedness, on the repressive rigour of her upbringing and her preparation for the fate of her mother — to have her hair shorn, to be subject to absurd laws of personal hygiene and behaviour, to be forced to watch from the women's gallery while her husband and sons celebrated the Sabbath in their prayer shawls and the marriage brokers turned over in their minds whom her daughters should marry. It had proved too much for her to bear even as a young girl so with a defiant gesture she had invited expulsion. 'So I left home and my father pronounced me dead, struck from the book of the living. But at least I am a free woman, mistress of my own fate, able to make my own decisions in life.' There was a long pause in which they could hear the fall and sifting of the ash from the glowing and fantastic castle of coal. 'I like the piece you brought me,' she said taking it up and rubbing the polished surface with her forefinger. 'There's a fossil in it,' he explained and held out his hand for the nugget. 'Look — it's a fern.' As he traced the delicate hairlines of the leaf she came closer to him. She was sitting on the hearth rug with her legs drawn up inside her skirt. Her head was close to his knee as she took the coal and looked down to examine the delicate tracery of the plant. He could see the delicate down at the back of her neck. There was a tiny mole on her neck just above the spot where a pulse beat gently. He stretched out a finger and stroked the skin between the collar of her high-necked blouse and the line of her hair. It was the same gesture as that with which he had traced the fronds of the fern in the coal. To his astonishment she arched her neck a little, offering it to his touch. Then she laid the coal in her lap and turning her head to him said: 'That was nice.' He was aware of an extraordinary surge of excitement that suffused his whole body; he felt an impulse to touch and a desire to be touched in return that was checked only by his fear. Faintly across the snow came the chime of the village clock striking two. It was echoed by the soft peal from the clock in its great glass case on the mantle-piece. She laughed. 'What is Mrs Ramsay going to say if you come home at this time in the morning?' He had a sudden access of doubt and insecurity, took her question literally and said something about having to go. In answer she laid her elbow on his knee and rested her head on it. 'Stroke me more,' she said and guided his hand to her neck. He felt the pulse beat under his touch as his fingers rested on her skin. She raised her hand to his and guided it down the front of her blouse to rest on her breast. He shivered at the feel of her flesh, warm and shifting beneath his touch. Suddenly he took his hand away and stood up. His abrupt movement caused her to slip down towards the floor. She picked herself up in a trice. 'What is this?' she cried. He stood with his arms dangling, sick and frightened. 'I do not have the right,' he began but she interrupted him with 'Perhaps I decide who can touch me or not.' With a suppliant gesture he held out a hand. 'You don't understand,' he said and was mute. 'I understand that you are afraid — or perhaps,' she added, 'for how am I to know? — there is something in me or even in all women that repels you and leaves you what you seem to be — a thirty-year-old virgin.' 'I am not a virgin,' he countered. 'Good,' she replied. 'But you behave like one — like an adolescent schoolboy.' He turned towards the door. 'I had better go,' he said but she was quicker than he and barred his way setting her back to the door. 'No. First you will explain to me what happened just now. You owe it to me.' He was silent, gripped by an inability to speak that froze his tongue and imposed a terrible dumbness. At last from his dry mouth he brought forth the reply that he could not find the words. There was always a way of finding words, she said firmly. He walked to and fro noticing irrelevantly but with intense clarity a loose thread on the edge of the carpet. He stooped down to pull it free. 'Well,' she challenged him. He turned and looked at her in despair. Once he opened his mouth as if about to talk but nothing came from it. At last he licked his lips with their bitter taste of dry spittle and began to speak about Perpignan, about Lebrun and Tante Marie's. When he had finished he stood and looked at the floor. He was shaking slightly. To his amazement he felt her take his hand and with a gentle pressure draw him towards the sofa. There she talked to him quietly. She knew something about these matters, she explained — from personal experience. She didn't wish to go into details but she knew what she was talking about. Then she began to question him and her questions were precise, clinical, diagnostic. At the end of her interrogation she laughed. 'What a Puritan conscience can do,' she said. 'You must get rid of your Puritanism — before it destroys you. You have heard my judgement. There is no need for fear. Do you accept it?' He nodded. 'But do you really?' she persisted. 'You must be clear. I require clarity and honesty in those who are close to me.' He spoke to her in a flood of joy that reached its climax when, in her bed, she touched his reclaimed and resurrected body.

He woke to the kind of muffled stillness which means that thick snow has fallen. There was a curious pale light on the unfamiliar ceiling. He turned in the strangely warm soft bed and found he was alone. There were no texts on the walls here. From the night before he remembered that a fire had burned in the grate. Raising himself a little he could see its cold ashes in the hearth. His clothes were on a chair at the foot of the bed. On a chaise-longue were a blouse and skirt and some pieces of underwear. On a table by the bed stood a photograph of a young man with thick hair brushed back from his face and a dark moustache; he wore a double-breasted coat with a fur collar that obscured part of his face. In a stand there were other photographs in which he recognized the two children and a man of about fifty who stood with his hands on their shoulders — a tall bearded man who gave an impression of confidence and assurance which contrasted with the defiance and stubbornness on the face of the young man whose picture stood alongside. When the door suddenly opened he took refuge in the bedclothes. Elizavyeta pulled them back with a laugh and announced breakfast; 'Coffee and toast.' She was wearing a dark red dressing gown with a laced collar. She rested the tray on the bedside table, pushing photographs to one side to make a space, and shaking the wide sleeves back from her wrists, began to pour the coffee. That done, to his astonishment she took off her dressing gown and sat naked in the bed beside him. 'I like breakfast in bed, don't you?' she asked. He had to admit that it was his first experience of it. 'I am going to write a book,' she announced, 'on the cultural deprivation of the

Scots. I have every right to. After all, when your ancestors were running about dressed in furs and painted blue in the fort up there, mine had discovered monotheism — which, people will tell you, was a great intellectual advance.' She laughed and drank her coffee slowly, dipping her toast in her cup. When she had finished she lay back in the pillows. 'That's my husband, Boris,' she said, pointing to the young man in the overcoat. 'He is in Siberia. I hear from him sometimes. Occasionally someone comes out of prison and into exile who has news of him. He has a long time to serve still — unless something explodes over there. And that is the children's father, Paul. He is very nice and kind. I could not have survived without his help.' There was a long pause. Then she took his plate and cup and laid them beside hers on the table. She slipped down between the bedclothes. She turned to him and looked seriously but lovingly into his face. 'There is one thing I won't have in anyone I am close to,' she said, 'that is jealousy.' Her hand stretched out to touch his body as if to emphasise their closeness. 'If they don't like it they can go.' The she said gaily: 'There are not trains today so you will have to stay till tomorrow. Which train will you arrive on? A late one or an early one? You needn't worry about Lienchen. We have been together a very long time. We understand each other.'

He stayed till the last train. He had not before in his life had the day and the night turned upside down and the business of life, of eating, sleeping, talking, reading, adapted to a time-table that was no timetable. He had never in his fantasies imagined that there could be such physical closeness, such an exchange of tenderness, such a seeking and finding, such intensity of feeling. When he walked back along Church Street and up to Mrs Ramsay's door he was almost light-headed. His landlady was full of expressions of concern, which he accepted with a slight feeling of guilt. But at least his story was credible — snow, cancelled trains, lost connections. He made no mention of his walk in the snow and his lift from the farmer. Young Adams would have had a skinful on New Year's Eve;

probably his horse found its own way home with him in the small hours. He was unlikely to remember much about the evening before. There was nothing to fear.

It would be interesting to speculate how within a community like Slateford it was possible for my father to carry on a liaison, a relationship, a love affair, a romance: whatever one cares to call it. Clearly the *convenances* would have to be respected and the relationship conducted in such a way as to avoid catching the eye of the village, so to speak, for its inhabitants were skilled to detect variations in behaviour, in habits, to note the time a man or a woman left the house, the route they took, the persons with whom they had contact. As headmaster John Scott was part of the establishment of the community, although his place in it was somewhat ambivalent, being lower by virtue of his appointment by the School Board than those who served on it but superior, because of his position and education, to the bulk of the villagers — superior in some respects even to the big farmers although they were elevated above him by their wealth and power. It followed that he was expected to present a model of behaviour not only to his pupils but to the village as a whole. Which is not to say that there were not in some of the villages in the countryside or in the glens with their tiny one-and two-teacher schools headmasters who were notorious for their capacity to put away the whiskey so that on Monday morning they would still be snarling from the hangover they had acquired on Saturday with the result that the tawse almost seemed to leap from their desks as they imposed order, punished real or fancied misdemeanours, and sought to overcome the headache and nausea that still lingered from the excesses of the weekend. But to be fond of a dram was different from conducting a sexual relationship with a woman of uncertain status and unknown antecedents. It was, of course, a society in which sex was widely practised: in haylofts when the single men from the bothies met the girls from the farmhouses at dusk; in the bracken of the woods as they walked home on summer evenings from a fair — like the Trinity horse-fair in June — or when the reaping was over in July or August; in winter after a dance in some barn where a fiddle and mouth-organ, supplemented perhaps by a twanging Jew's harp, made the music for reels and strathspeys and the dust rose from the dancer's feet to swirl in the light of the lantern hung from a cross-beam. It was not by chance that Slateford was only some fifteen miles from Kirriemuir, the scene of that great ball — in truth a ploughman's barn dance —which is celebrated in a famous bawdy folk-song. Sidney Goodsir Smith rightly describes it in his introduction to Robert Burns's own collection of 'bawdy folk-songs, ancient and modern' — *The Merry Muses of Caledonia* — as the flowering of this great art form. He locates the event it describes in the 1880s. One summer, after the 'hairst' — the harvest — the young men came with their caps over the ears and an intricate plaited favour made of a dry corn stalk in their buttonholes and scattered — so the story goes — seeds of the ripe rose-hips on the packed earth of the floor where the girls with their long dresses and loose open drawers danced barefoot. The beat of their feet on the floor raised clouds of dust laden with the tiny hairy seeds which clung like burrs to skin and hair under the girls' skirts as they swung on their partners' arms in the reels. The paraffin lamp suddenly flickered and went out; someone had stuffed it with a divot of grass that absorbed the fuel. The musicians played on, sitting in a corner with a bottle of whiskey handy to slake their drouthy mouths. But in the dark the bacchanalia had begun as the aphrodisiac itch of the seed grew on the tender exposed flesh. It was a night commemorated in a song that began in the bothies where the single men cooked their supper of meal and potatoes, that acquired new verses and accretions, that knew variants and strange readings, but which had always the same pounding refrain:

Saying fa'll dae it this time
Fa'll dae it noo

The yin that did it last time
Canna dae it noo.

Willie Hamilton sang it on the troopship that took him out to the Cape to fight the Boers. Two world wars diffused the ballad far beyond the farmsteads where it was first sung. It was a commonplace item in the improvised concerts on the troopships as they trundled slowly through the milky incandescent tropical seas with their cargoes of soldiers of whom, on a simple calculation of probabilities, a third would not come back. It was sung in NAAFI tents and canteens in Cairo or in the great brothel quarter of the Berka: the scene of a sadder sexual ritual as the men queued for such pleasures as they could afford with the women — Greek, Maltese, Sudanese, Egyptian, Jewish — who satisfied and mocked the desires of the new drafts, pale-faced, fresh out from England, or veterans of the desert with their faces and bodies burnt brown by the sun and wind of Libya and, at the back of their minds, giving an added edge to their lust, the consciousness of death avoided, of death perhaps waiting in the minefields around Tobruk. But if sex was acknowledged and indeed celebrated in the male society of the armies, if Willie Hamilton could, when he was loquacious with drink, tell of black women and brown women and the brothels of Cape Town, in the day-to-day life of Slateford its existence was publicly denied; which did not mean it was banished from the minds of the men and women who saw, gossiped, speculated at the changed tenor of life of their headmaster who was now — as they put it — 'carrying on' with a foreign woman.

John told her of the ballad and the orgy it celebrated one Saturday when the tutoring was over and the children had run off across the fields to explore the woods and search for the first willow catkins — pussy willows with their flowers like soft cats' paws. Lienchen had gone to take her afternoon siesta,

126

it being one of the stratagems of their lovemaking that the time for weekly tutoring had been moved to the afternoon so that there was no need for him to hurry back for Mrs Ramsay's lunch; so they lay together and laughed as he translated the verses from the local dialect with its substitution of f for wh — fa for who, faur for where, fan for when. Fa'll dae it this time, fa'll dae it noo' he sang softly in her ear as with his fingers he explored the silken skin of the cavity where her thigh joined her pelvis. She said she didn't know, kissed him and said she had nothing to offer in return for she didn't really know many Russian folk-songs — at least not that kind — though no doubt they existed and no doubt men sang them in the Siberian camps as they sat round the table in the long wooden huts with the stove roaring and the Arctic wind whistling under the door. But there was a poem by a Russian poet called Blok which suggested the same kind of provincial sexuality and she quoted the verse about how the young bloods, their hats at a jaunty angle, stroll with their girls beyond the level crossing and how the moon looks down with a wry smile on the lake where from the boats there comes the creak of rowlocks and the cry of a woman's voice. It was a poem, she reflected, that should appeal to a Scot ending as it does with the apparition of a mysterious veiled figure, an unknown woman, who each evening passes close to the table where the poet sits, drinks by himself and discovers through her agency hidden treasures in his heart. 'But I forgot,' she said laughing and bringing her body closer to his, 'that you are a Puritan who does not drink and does not like making love.'

Given the cast of mind of the society in which the two lovers found themselves and the public visibility of John Scott as headmaster I cannot help feeling that the opportunities they had to spend any time together — far less a night in the same bed — must have been infrequent. This makes me think that one of the reasons which prompted him to move into the schoolhouse when it was completed in the early spring was the possibility of pursuing the relationship more easily, although the house itself was exposed, being next to the Free Church and only a couple of doors down from Mrs Ramsay. She was genuine in her regret over his leaving for mixed reasons: one was that she had come to like him, although she had noticed a certain distance between them of late, and the other that she was deprived by his departure of a certain prestige in the village and was no longer able in the butcher's or the grocer's or in the post office to make assertions on a variety of subjects, ranging from educational policy to the attendance rate at school, with the confidence of one who could suggest that she was in the confidence of the dominie. The advantages offered by the schoolhouse were privacy and the fact that in the tall sandstone wall that sealed off the kitchen garden — or what one day might become it — there was a gate into a lane which in turn led into the field path leading to the villa. To some extent then passage to and fro by one or other of the lovers was easier, although it was he who usually walked over, for he knew that the eyes of the village might catch them — in the early morning the baker's boy delivering rolls, the milk-maid with her pails, or a farmer from a smallholding in the village up and about for some task in the fields. After school he at least had the excuse that he had some errand connected with his duties as a tutor, so he would carry under his arm a couple of books or some jotters, as if he were going to discuss their written homework. It is true that he now had a housekeeper recommended by the Reverend James Murdoch, a widow woman who lived in a cottage on the edge of the Muir but who did for him during the day, leaving once he had had his supper. So in the evening — at least until the long northern twilights began — there was little fear of discovery. In daytime, at the weekends, I imagine they made trysts to which they travelled separately by bicycle riding north of the village, for example, and then turning west past the isolated village graveyard and the red ruined castle of the Lindsays to the upper reaches of the West Water. Here they would leave their bicycles in the high broom above the river, cross the ravine through which it flowed by a narrow plank bridge and so walk upstream to the falls, where in spring the salmon shot up through the spray like silver spears as they drove towards the spawning grounds in the gravel reaches at the head of the stream. Here they would lie in sheltered hollows on a hillside among the young heather and bracken and watch the clouds saunter through the sky. It must have been difficult for them to get away together, although they contrived a visit to London. That must have been in the Easter holidays. They discussed the possibility first at a meeting in the pine woods south of the village. It was a Saturday. He had gone off early to the market town on his bicycle to pick up a book from the stationer's — Carlyle's *Sartor Resartus* — and a pound of home-made toffees from the little shop off the High Street. He had timed his journey so that at about eleven he was in the woods where he dismounted, laid his bicycle in the bracken and walked further into the trees along a track the woodsmen had cleared for their long carts. The path under his feet was covered by a thick coating of slippery brown pine-needles. The wood was quiet however and no felling was going on. There was the cheep of a tree-creeper and the tiny call of a wren. A branch creaked now and then as the breeze moved the tree-tops. He found her as they had arranged on the slopes of a curious hill which once, before the pines were planted, must have dominated the village and been visible for miles around; tradition said that it had once been the hanging hill when the Lindsays had the right of 'pit and gallows'. She was halfway down the hill kneeling in the bracken. When she saw him she waved urgently so that he ran up from the path. She was bending over a rabbit caught in a trap. It lay with its ears laid back in terror and its eyes fixed in a stare of fear. The trap had shattered a hindleg. It no longer struggled. When he laid a hand on the beast its only reaction was a convulsion that ran through the whole body and a slight movement of the head. 'I've tried to open it,' she said, 'but it won't move.' He knew there must be some simple way to release the trap but he could see no obvious lever or pin and although he tugged at the steel jaws they remained firmly shut on shattered bone and torn fur. 'There is only one way,' she said. 'It has to be killed.' 'How?' he asked. 'You break its neck,' she replied. 'I can't,' he objected. She said nothing but stroked the animal gently and then grasping the head firmly jerked it back. He could hear the spine crack. A last tremor ran through the body which then lay limp and warm to the touch. 'There are times,' she said, 'when you have to be decisive and even cruel. Or so I have learned.' He felt her words as a threat to himself and to their closeness — a sudden flood of fear that robbed him of words. She climbed ahead of him to the top of the knoll where they sat down. From a pocket in her skirt she produced one of her tiny cheroots and lit it. 'Why are you so quiet?' she asked blowing a puff of smoke into a cloud of midges. 'Have I shocked you?' He prevaricated. Not really, he had seen his mother kill hens in the days when they had an allotment but he had never been able to do it himself. 'Some people have to learn. Maybe you will have to learn one day. Now Major MacIllroy knows how to kill and would kill without hesitation if he thought it necessary. But I doubt if it will ever be necessary here.' She smoked quietly for a little and then looked into his face. He was uncomfortable and attempted to disguise it by playing with a pine cone which he tossed into the air and caught again. 'Maybe you have a problem. I know what it is. You want everything to be nice but that is not the way the world is made or the way people are.' He did not answer but threw the cone up again; this time she interposed her hand and caught it. For the first time he felt an impulse of anger. But she dispelled it with a touch of her hand. 'Don't be upset,' she said. 'I wanted to discuss a plan — a good one. I have to go to London at Easter. Would you like to come with me?' Joyfully he agreed. They would travel separately to Perth and pick up the London train there. In London she had friends who would put them up.

So they went to London and he learned something of what life was like as an exile, voluntary or involuntary. Elizavyeta's friends lived near King's Cross in a row of houses that were run-down and on the verge of becoming slums but still preserved something of their stylish past in their bow-fronted windows and the high-ceilinged rooms. Outside children played noisily on the pavement, stopping occasionally to watch the comings and goings of the foreigners who led their strange lives within. The friends were a Russian couple who, having established that John was not political, took little notice of him. It was a difficult time for him. Elizavyeta was occupied with meetings and discussions lasting far into the night from which he was excluded by language and by what seemed to him to be their hosts' obsessive insistence on secrecy. There were compensations, it was true, in that when he had fallen asleep to the sound of foreign debates he would be wakened by the coolness of her skin as she slipped into bed and put her arm round him for warmth. After such late sessions she would sleep late; he lay beside her and read, waiting for her to emerge from sleep. Then they would make love. At first he was inhibited by the thought that the couple who were their hosts must guess what kept Elizavyeta and himself in bed so long and was shy of appearing in the kitchen where they sat round a samovar, smoking, reading newspapers, eating sporadically and displaying complete indifference to the squalor that surrounded them. He had known poverty or at least strained circumstances, but even in the tenements of Stirling he had not seen such indifference to dirt and disorder. Elizavyeta laughed at his shyness and sympathized with his dislike of the grime and the dirty dishes. But one had to make allowances, she explained, for people whose energies were limited and whose priorities were not those of domesticity. In any case their own room was very presentable; which was true for she had bought flowers and a couple of coloured prints which he found vivid and disturbing. The window gave on to a patch of grass and in the morning the room was full of sun. He lay in bed and watched her wash at the basin marvelling at the line of her back and the soft roundness of her thighs. Sometimes he would rise up from bed and they would embrace and feel the sun on their bodies as they turned back once more to mingle their limbs and continue that unending process of exploration on which they were both embarked.

But much of his time he spent alone in the British Museum.

He found the classical sculptures disappointing — cramped and grey and unlike his vision of classical Greece or Rome. He preferred the rooms where poisoned arrows, Indian head-dresses, clubs and wooden Maori axes were crammed in long glass-fronted cupboards along with snowshoes, beads and Eskimo furs. It was a mixture that fascinated him because of an object glimpsed among the jumble — a cape of humming-bird feathers or an obsidian axe — but made little sense otherwise. In the Egyptian rooms he saw the mummified cats and ibises and looked into a sarcophagus to see the body of a man, dry and brown like leather. When he came back someone was bound to ask him whether he had been in the Library and whether he had seen the place where Karl Marx used to sit. At least three different people told the story about the attendant who, on being shown a portrait of Marx said yes, he knew the face but he hadn't seen him about for a while. At this they all laughed before switching to Russian or German to continue the interminable discussions in which Elizavyeta would join, smoking her long cheroot. He felt alone, excluded and vaguely afraid, as if he were standing on the edge of something he did not understand but which was explosive, dangerous and alien. Sometimes he would sit reading in the kitchen while they discussed in the room next door. From time to time one of them would emerge from its cramped, smokey space and apparently without noticing his existence fetch water for the samovar, the strange tea-urn they kept continually replenished, continually on the boil.

They were men and women of all ages and, apparently of different social origins, from what might have been university lecturers to workmen: a judgement which Elizavyeta confirmed. He found it difficult to believe that these men and women were confident that they would one day bring down empires, overthrow tyrannies and build a totally new society in their place. For that they seemed too ordinary, too unremarkable. Yet Elizavyeta was able to point to this man who had been a prisoner in the Fortress of Peter and Paul in St Petersburg while the young woman with her hair arranged in two coils over her ears was Polish and had served prison sentences for revolutionary activities in the textile town of Lodz. Perhaps it was their ordinariness that made it difficult for him seriously to accept at its face value their fanatical security which, on one occasion, meant that he had to remain shut up in the bedroom because an important emissary from Russia was expected whom he must not even see and, on others, caused them to go through complicated stratagems to shake off the agents who, they were persuaded, followed them through the streets, on the buses and on the Metropolitan line. Only when Elizavyeta told him that one of their number had been summarily deported and was now, no doubt, in the hands of the secret police, the Okhrana, did he begin to believe that their paranoia might be justified.

Sometimes when he sat alone in the bedroom he thought of making his way to the Pool of London to see his brother; but then decided against it. There was nothing to be gained from a meeting and the subsequent and inevitable inquisition. But there were other, better times when Elizavyeta contrived to liberate herself. So one afternoon in spring sunlight they walked on Primrose Hill, watched children flying kites and people exercising their dogs, from which to his surprise he had to defend Elizavyeta who clutched his arm as the beasts gambolled harmlessly up the hill. From the top they looked across to the Surrey Hills and picked out landmarks: St Paul's, the churches of the City, Big Ben, the roof of the Albert Hall, the shot tower on the south bank of the Thames. She said she had heard about the view from the hill from a friend of her husband's — that same Ulyanov who had been a member of the student group at the Technical High School and who, like Marx, had spent his time in London in the library of the British Museum, working on a book about imperialism. Now he was living near Paris under another name and running a political school. She knew him through a friend of hers, Inessa Armand, whom she usually looked up when she was in Paris. She thought the two were very close, very fond of each other, but didn't think they actually had an affair. Think what they are missing, she added, squeezing his arm affectionately before, with one of the spontaneous gestures which both delighted and embarrassed him, she ran off to the bottom of the slope where an entirely un-aggressive Airedale brought her to a halt. Once out in Regent's Park Road she insisted in walking up and down, scanning the houses that gave on to the park, in an attempt to determine where it was that Friedrich Engels had lived. 'He should interest you,' she explained, during her search, 'he lived with a young woman who claimed to be descended from Robert Burns.' In the end she was still undecided but of one thing she was sure: he must read Engels' *Socialism Utopian and Scientific*, which was in her view and in the view of many of the comrades — a word that fell strangely on his ears — quite simply the best and clearest introduction to socialist theory.

Another day she took him to the National Gallery, leading him with a sure sense of purpose through one room after another with barely a glance at their contents, to confront him with Rembrandt's self-portrait in old age wearing a red jacket with a fur collar and with his hands clasped before him. He had no experience to set beside his first sight of that grave, sad face. Up to now he had always thought that painting was to do with illustrating a story, evoking a landscape which might be gay or sombre, or reproducing something obviously pleasurable like a bunch of flowers. Here was a picture almost as brown as the late Mr Ramsay's but of incomparable power. 'If I were a painter,' said Elizavyeta as they walked out into Trafalgar Square, 'I would want to be brave enough to paint a picture of myself as honest and as fearless as Rembrandt's.' He said nothing but I believe he may have carried that image in his mind for the rest of his life, particularly when he himself was old and caught a glimpse of his own time-battered face in a mirror or in the glass of a shop-window.

When I was twelve we went to London — went by boat from Dundee, a three day voyage down the east coast to land in Limehouse and make our way parsimoniously on foot to the tube in Whitechapel past the shops of Chinatown, of Limehouse, and the Jewish shops with their strange script, to an hotel where, if my mother were to be believed, unmentionable disease lurked on every lavatory seat. One morning, having followed the Horse Guards through the August heat up Constitution Hill to Horse Guards Parade we dragged on after the guard mounting was over across Trafalgar Square and into the National Gallery. I remembered of it only walls of pictures, some of which I might have liked to stop and examine, others which I passed in wearied incomprehension until at last we came to a halt in front of quite a small picture of an old man wearing a curious bonnet. His hair was grey and fuzzy and rather long. He had a thin grey moustache and a curious tuft of hair on his chin. His reddish jacket had a fur collar and a big leather button a few inches below it. 'That's a funny kind of jacket for a man to be wearing,' commented my mother. There was a pause in which my father made no remark. 'It's not the sort of thing I'd want in my house,' my mother went on. My father was still silent. I looked at the wrinkles under the man's eyes and was suddenly frightened by an overwhelming sense of sadness. I tugged at my mother's sleeve. 'Can't we go,' I whispered. 'John,' she said, 'you're not going to stand here all day, I hope. The laddie's worn out with trailing about in the heat. It's time we had a bite to eat.' My father turned without a word. I was curious because he was not angry but looked solemn and a bit sad. We had lunch in a Lyons Corner House. I had my first mixed grill although my mother was sure it would make me sick. But my father said to let me be to enjoy things when I could.

On their second last day in London something happened which he had always known to be a possibility, however remote. Stepping off a bus in the Strand they found his brother waiting at the stop. In Tom's greeting there was a mixture of genuine pleasure, surprise and curiosity. 'Tom,' said his brother, 'may I introduce you to Miss de Pass.' 'Miss de Pass,' said Tom, 'I take it you parlez frangsay.' John squirmed but Elizavyeta smiled and said she did and added that she had learned a lot about him from John. As they moved off together — there was clearly no way of getting rid of him — Tom nudged John with his elbow and whispered in his ear: 'Going steady, then, are you?' John blushed and did not answer. 'Where should we have lunch?' she asked, 'I'm sure you know a good place.' Tom led them along the Strand and into Fleet Street. There was an eating-house there that served proper English fare, steak and kidney pudding — had Miss de Pass ever had real steak and kidney pudding? — and a glass of good ale. The place was crowded but Tom was quick to find places and handed Elizavyeta into her seat with a bow that was only half-mocking. As they waited for their order she began to talk to Tom, questioning him about his firm: what countries did they trade with? in what commodities? what did he think the firm's annual turnover might be? what were the dockers paid? how were they hired? and what were his own prospects? In his answers Tom revealed to his brother a side of his nature of which he had up to now been ignorant; for if Tom was surprised at first he was soon talking with confidence and knowledge about the trade in timber with the Baltic ports, the price of jute from Calcutta, using terms like demurrage and c.i.f. and putting forward views that the firm, which was really a Scottish firm founded in the eighteenth century, badly needed an injection of capital and new management to shake it up a bit, which he would welcome because it would probably mean promotion and the possibility of being chief clerk one day. She should come down and see the wharf; which she did after their meal, which Tom insisted on paying for, picking her way among the dray-horses and asking questions incessantly.

At the door of the office with its big brass plate *The Baltic Trading and Shipping Company Ltd* they parted. 'It has been a real pleasure,' said Tom, removing his hat, 'a real pleasure.' Turning to John he clapped him on the arm: 'You should have told me, old man. Drop me a line will you? Don't forget.' Then he was off jumping up the stairs two at a time. 'That was interesting,' said Elizavyeta as they walked back over the railway tracks and through to London Bridge. 'He's not stupid, your brother. He'll do well under capitalism.'

Tom did not have time to do well under capitalism. Enlisting in the London Scottish in 1914 he said goodbye to Piccadilly and farewell to Leicester Square with a certain nonchalance, came back on leave to Stirling before leaving for France, looking fine in his kilt, his mother wrote to John, but was quiet and untalkative. Within the year he was dead. One of a thin line of men, he walked across no-man's land behind a creeping barrage with his rifle and his entrenching tool and a coil of barbed wire, leaning forwards and stooping as if facing a strong wind. He got as far as the German wire. It was uncut. The barrage had passed on implacably to other targets. From somewhere to the flank a German machine gun opened up enfilading the wire. They found his body later — one of the long swathe of dead men lying rank upon rank. A couple of years ago, being at a summer school, I looked at a war memorial in Stirling and saw his name, which is also my own. I found it again in the little village churchyard not far away where my father and mother and my grandfather and various aunts and uncles lie beneath the polished red granite headstone.

They arrived back at Slateford separately. He felt sad and lonely on the journey back. Their parting at Euston station, their last embrace before he rose to dress in the early morning, had struck him as rehearsals for another parting, which he felt must lie before them and to which he was almost resigned. When or how he did not know. All he could be certain of was that parting there would be. The thought of it shot through even their happiest moments together and brought tears to his eyes when they lay close, as close as two human bodies can hope to lie. Easter was early that year so that when they met again there were still patches of snow in some of the sheltered corries in the hills above the village even if down by the West Water the willows were already putting out their catkins, soft and grey like the pads of a rabbit's foot. He cut her a bunch one Saturday and brought it with him when he arrived to teach the children. She took it with joy and explained how in Russia, in the Orthodox Church, the catkins and the palm leaf were conjoined as symbols of Easter. He for his part suggested that they colour Easter eggs with the flower of the whin, with onion skins or coffee grounds. Then they must roll them downhill as a symbol of the rolling away of the stone from the tomb. She laughed and reminded him that she was not and never had been a Christian. In any case she preferred to think that the custom derived from some pagan fertility rite with which to celebrate spring and mating. One thing they both found difficult now that they were back: the need to behave in a restrained way in front of the children, although it was impossible totally to obscure the closeness that had grown between them. With the children he had made some progress in terms of their ability to read and write English, which she remarked laughingly they spoke with a Scottish accent. But beyond that he had not progressed. They were both intelligent — not more so, he reflected, than some of the boys and girls in his top class — but it was as if they resented him. Elizavyeta discussed their resentment in oedipal terms. He found the theory far fetched and unconvincing but had no explanation to offer himself for the undercurrent of negative feelings he had come to expect from them. He must understand, she explained, even if he did not accept the Oedipus legend and its application to their case, that they felt very isolated in Slateford and that they did not see the point in learning English, given that they already spoke French and German. They didn't understand, she added with a smile, that one must know the languages of both the great powers, the two empires which would shortly face each other in a struggle for world domination. One or other of them would emerge victorious from the rivalry in which they were now caught up: building warships, competing for markets, forming political alliances. So English *and* German it had to be. What about French then? he added. Ah, French, she replied, French would remain the language of the spirit, of the mind — whatever he cared to call it — and as such essential, the lingua franca of the intelligentsia.

He still wondered about the roots of Rachel's indifferent civility and David's sullen resentment. It was a question that led him to ponder over Elizavyeta's relationship to Paul; after long hesitation he found the courage to question her about it. She answered without embarrassment and with clarity, both reactions which he by now ought to have expected from her; but he was still slightly surprised by her frankness. Paul was an old friend who had helped her in various ways: when she was studying in Berlin, when she was ill and had to go to the mountains in Switzerland, when she had almost lost hope. They no longer had what she described in a curious term as 'a love relationship' but were still bound by respect and affection being (that phrase again) very fond of each other. That was why she had agreed to keep the children for some months while he was abroad — in the United States and in South America — making business contacts for his chemical firm. John was puzzled at her regard for a businessman who was part of what she would call the capitalist system. Whereupon she took him to task for thinking in simplistic terms. They did not have socialism yet and people had to live. He was a good, intelligent man who reminded her a bit of Engels, that businessman and manufacturer who used his wealth to finance Marx. In the same way Paul was convinced that the economic system of which he was part was fundamentally unjust; he was wealthy but his wealth — or some of it — went to help men and women of the Left who were in difficulties, ill, or needed finances for their struggle: to print a journal, for example, or to bring delegates to a conference in Berlin or London. He would be back from America in the summer when the children would rejoin him in London or Berlin. John's heart sank. Did that mean she would leave too?

It was evening. They were lying in bed in the schoolhouse, which he had furnished somewhat inadequately. She did not reply immediately but began to talk about how he might arrange the rooms, although he would have to wait till he was married since his wife would no doubt have views too. He protested at her picture of his future, which he resented for the calm way in which it assumed separation; she rebuked him in a gentle way, telling him not to be silly, that it was so and must be so. 'You haven't answered my question,' he countered. 'No,' she agreed, 'But when I do I will try to let you know in plenty of time.' Then she looked down at his naked body and said inconsequentially; 'I can't get over the fact that you are not a Jew.' She laughed. 'I've never had a lover before who wasn't a Jew.' He lay there looking glum. She shook him playfully and laid her hand on his penis. 'You mustn't sulk. You must see life as it is. You may not have had other women but I have had other men friends and I do not conceal the fact from you. In any case did I make a fuss when you told me about the girl in Tante Marie's?' Then he was teased out of his petulance and turned to her.

It was early in the summer term. In school the top classes were busy with what he called a project, an attempt to relate learning to life and practice: building a wheel-barrow for the school garden which had been broken out in a corner of a field behind the school. There were a number of stages to the project. The first involved the production of scale isometric drawings of the barrow. Then the cost of the materials had to be calculated, after which the boys and girls went out in groups to the joiner and the blacksmith to discover the cost of the timber and of making the iron rim for the wheel. Frank

Low led the group to the smithy where they bargained with the blacksmith amid the smell of singed hooves and the clamour of the hammers on the anvil. The children had just returned and were reporting their findings, which the headmaster was writing on the blackboard when there was a knock at the classroom door. Standing there was a groom from the Burnfoot who had come in the pony and trap to deliver a letter: 'With Major MacIllroy's compliments.' The headmaster thanked him and enquired whether a reply was needed. The groom said No and turned away. The headmaster laid the envelope with its inscription to John Scott, Esq., M.A. on his desk and continued the lesson; but his attention was not as wholehearted as before; on some pretext he broke off the lesson till next day and told the children to go to their seats and read silently. He opened the letter, cutting the paper cleanly, precisely with his penknife. It said that the Major presented his compliments and would be obliged if Mr Scott would call on him at the Burnfoot at 8.30 pm to discuss a matter of some importance and gravity.

After school, over the indifferent high tea served by his housekeeper, the headmaster turned over in his mind what the important and grave matter might be. He had a cold feeling in his chest, a kind of sick numbness, that robbed him of all appetite. At the back of his mind the certainty formed that it was to do with Elizavyeta. No doubt the source of the trouble was once again Miss Kerr; but that was a minor matter. The fact was that something which he had in a sense thought of as apart from and outside his normal life had entered the public sphere where his existence and career were at stake. When he mounted his bicycle and set off up the High Street on the mile-long ride to the Burnfoot he still felt cold inside but his coldness had changed into a determination to face whatever accusations might be made and to stand by his right to his relationship with a woman whom he loved. He was a bachelor who had a right to friendship with a woman. That she had a husband in some camp in Siberia they were not likely to know.

He crossed the stone bridge over the East Water and turned

in at the lodge-gate to the Burnfoot. The lodge-keeper looked out and bade him good evening. The drive went up between tall beech trees and led him to a broad gravel space before the house, which was classical with Doric pillars and a cupola in the centre of the roof. When he rang the bell a solemn butler answered, ushered him in and announced in an affectedly English voice that he would inform the Major that Mr Scott had arrived. On the walls of the hall there were dark and obscure portraits of men in Highland garb or Scottish regimentals, leaning on claymores or contemplating some field of battle. There were ladies too, pale and delicate most of them, with loose scarves that concealed their bosoms and hair piled high on their heads. Between the paintings were crossed swords and Highland targes and a couple of flintlock pistols.

The butler was away a long time. He emerged from the back of the house with a sign to the headmaster to follow him down a long corridor with stone flags underfoot until they reached a room where the Major was busy cleaning and oiling a shot-gun. From the way the room was cluttered with fishing tackle and shooting gear it was clear that this was the Major's special territory. When the headmaster entered a large red retriever rose with its tongue dangling and gave a slight growl but it subsided at a word from the Major, who gave a cursory greeting and went on pulling a rag through the barrel, appeared satisfied and laid the gun gently in its case. 'A Purdey,' he commented. 'But I don't suppose you know what that means. I had it from my father and if I had a son it would have been his. Anyway, let's not beat about the bush, Mr Scott. As I indicated in my letter I have to discuss with you a matter of some gravity. To come straight to the point it concerns your relationship with a certain lady in Slateford. Now to be quite blunt I don't know whether you are fucking her or not. In a sense it is not my business whom you fuck — I'm talking to you as one man to another, after all we're not children — but it is my business when, as chairman of the School Board I receive a formal complaint to the effect that the headmaster of the village school — for which in a sense I am responsible — is carrying on an affair with a lady who may or may not be married, whose antecedents are, to say the least of it vague, and whose connections are curious. But I thought I would do the decent thing and instead of putting you on the mat at the next Board meeting just have a word between ourselves. Well?' The headmaster was silent. His mouth was dry and yet he felt a curious cold certainty forming his reply. 'Well then, man, lost your voice or something? Why can't you speak up?' The Major had measured out a quantity of snuff on the back of his hand and as he waited for an answer inhaled it deeply, shook his head slightly, sneezed and then, producing a huge red handkerchief from the pocket of his Norfolk jacket, noisily blew his nose. As he did so he looked questioningly at the teacher, who opened his mouth and began to speak.

He began from the beginning — explaining how he had been engaged to tutor the two children, how he had come to know and like Miss de Pass, how they had become friends so that now — the phrase came to his lips instinctively — they were 'very fond of each other'. The Major grunted. As far as he was concerned they could be as fond of each other as they liked and he didn't pay over much attention to old wives' tales, but there was the village clergy to be considered, there were the feelings of the villagers whose children went to the village school to be instructed — not just how to make a wheel-barrow, which seemed to be their main education at the moment — but in religion and moral behaviour. His own view was that clergymen should visit the sick, provide charity for those who needed it and preach on Sunday but not meddle in matters that were really none of their business. But the headmaster knew the score as well as he did. This was Slateford and not some European resort where no one minded too much who went to bed with whom. He'd been on the Continent, too, and knew what went on. But there was a limit. One had to draw a line somewhere. And it looked to him as if the time had come to draw it. So what had Mr Scott to say.

To his own astonishment Mr Scott heard himself say that he could always resign if it came to that. But the Major told him not to be daft. Whereupon the headmaster said that he did not feel that he could give any guarantees that he would not see Miss de Pass or continue his friendship with her. He was unmarried — what about the lady? interjected the Major — and the lady was free to follow her inclinations. He really had no more to say. 'So it's a case of all for love,' said the Major. 'Well, I'll say this for you — you at least have the guts to stick to your guns.' He walked up and down the room a couple of times. 'I tell you what, Mr Scott. I'll quash the matter this time. But I can't answer for the ministers of the Board. But for God's sake, be discreet at least.' He went over to a cupboard and produced a bottle of whiskey and a couple of glasses. 'I expect you could do with a glass. It's a single malt and probably wasted on you but it's my favourite tipple.' He filled up the glasses; this time the headmaster did not refuse. '*Sliant*,' said the Major and sipped the liquor, which was pale and tasted slightly of peat. Then he pulled a bell-rope which fetched the butler.

Outside it was dark and quiet. Beyond the grounds there was the rush and crash of water on the falls above the bridge. The air as the headmaster cycled back was cool and sobering. He shivered slightly because of the cold and because of the sudden uncertainty in which his life must now be lived. When he rode into the village street and left the open spaces of the Muir behind him the clock struck quarter to ten. He decided to ignore the Major's advice about discretion and to go straight to the villa. The light was burning in the study as usual; this time he did not have to wait for an answer to his ringing for Elizavyeta was there almost immediately having guessed who it must be. In hurried and elliptical terms which made her stop him from time to time to get the story clear he recounted the events of the day, adding the suspicion that the complaint must have come from Miss Kerr. Elizavyeta listened in silence to the account of the conversation with the Major; at the end of it she laughed. 'Good for the Major,' she said. But he was an enemy in her view of society, John objected. She laughed again: I've told you before — if all our political enemies were nasty people life would be so much easier. Dear John, you want everything in life to be nice and simple — but life is not like that. It is full of contradictions — as is politics. What you are telling me is a proof of the complications of relationships within our society. Like everyone else the Major is full of contradictions. In this case the contradiction works in your favour. Wasn't there some ridiculous rule in the British Army that young officers could not get married under the age of twenty-eight — or was it thirty? How did he know that the Major had not himself had a 'relationship' with a woman which had been thwarted in some stupid way? In any case, suppose the worst came to the worst and the matter did come up at the next Board meeting which was when? In a week's time? Then he must take a stand and force them to sack him. There was no need to be noble and resign. In any case, if it did come to that he could always make a living. He had only to think of all those refugees in London who would have to learn English whether they wanted to or not and who wouldn't mind in the least if they acquired a Scottish accent at the same time. Beyond that there was a whole community in Geneva. She could introduce him and she was sure Paul would help if there were immediate financial difficulties. In any case the situation was far from desperate. He agreed but he did not have her experience of life, could not — or at least not yet — accept that it was possible to live so contingent an existence. Somewhere not quite conscious but not entirely hidden, like a twinge from a tooth that came and went, was a node of fear and indecision. For the time being he was able to obliterate it in her embrace.

Major MacIllroy's case I think of as worse than she imagined. Commissioned into his father's regiment he had joined them in Bangalore. He had been a good subaltern, drilling with his men under the eye of the regimental sergeant-major one morning a week, dancing Highland reels on the parade ground on two mornings, and on the others going through parade-ground manoeuvres which had last been useful at the time of Wellington. He knew his men well and nourished a certain affection for them — much as one might for a faithful hound — while referring to them as 'the sweaty Jocks.' In his spare time he shot sand grouse or, on furlough, put up duck from the jeels in Kashmir; there were places too where the peacocks would come hurtling over the treetops and on to the guns like oversize pheasants. He lay in wait at waterholes for wart-hog and once, on a princely estate, had a shot at a tiger but just missed. In the mess he played cards for modest stakes and drank no more than the rest of his fellow officers, paid his mess bills regularly and was generally set for a predictable career. A campaign on the Frontier gave him a medal and an MC for rushing a Pathan sangar; then came promotion to lieutenant and shortly after to the brevet rank of captain. Women interested him little. For sex there were the chi-chi girls, the Anglo-Indians, with their fine profiles, full breasts and high-pitched accents, who were available at the Queen's Hotel on the edge of the regimental lines. Here the young officers would go to drink and break up the furniture and find their way up the back-stairs to the parlour where the girls waited, smelling of patchouli, dancing together to pass the time to the accompaniment of an old pianola, quick and smiling in their welcome, practised in bed. Then riding one day on the maidan, he met and fell in love with the wife of the new medical officer. For one reason or another she was bored with her husband, who drank too much or was not interested in sex. Who it was that reported him to his commanding officer he never discovered. To avoid scandal he was posted hurriedly to staff college from which he emerged in time to join the staff of General Redvers Buller in the Cape and to witness a display of military incompetence that almost lost Britain the war. His father dying — fortunately the scandal had been kept from him — he returned to take over the Burn estate, preserving with a certain vanity the rank of Major although technically he was only a captain. He was not too old to serve in the Great War and may well have been that officer who at the Somme was seen walking to and fro on the parapet of the trench along with a piper, encouraging the men to clamber out of the trenches — these men who had been ploughmen, carters, grieves, cattlehands, woodmen in the strath round Slateford and whom now he watched walk slowly forward behind the barrage. When they were pinned by the German fire he walked out to where they lay, rallied the survivors and went ahead of them to the line of trenches where a handgrenade tore his chest open. Since he died without issue the estate passed to a nephew who allowed Miss MacIllroy to live on in a kind of dower house while the property slowly ran down and the trees were cut and sold.

I knew just such a man as Major MacIllroy, brave, stupid but curiously understanding of his men and his fellow officers. In the Cauldron battle in Libya in the early summer of 1942 I visited his battalion headquarters, saw from the situation map in the Intelligence Officer's truck how he had led his company across the flat desert and on to Rommel's dug-in tanks and machine-guns. It was a battle for which he was totally unprepared against an enemy which outmatched him in experience and tactics. I saw the survivors returning, pale, shaken and unable to speak. He had been killed early on. He had been with the commanding officer when the advance was held up by heavy fire. There was a hurried conference at the end of which, having received his orders, he stood up and saluted. At that moment, as he turned to go, a bullet struck him between the eyes.

It was with some misgivings that the headmaster walked in to the village hall and took his seat at the committee table for the Board meeting during the week after his talk with the Major. He did not know what to expect — an attack of some kind but on what issue he did not know. It came from the parish minister who opened up saying: 'Mr Scott, I am reliably informed that you have abandoned traditional teaching practices and have set the pupils in the top classes to work on what I believe you describe as 'a project'. The headmaster felt immediate relief; if that was the chosen ground for battle he could defend himself on professional grounds. 'I should like to remind you, headmaster, speaking always through the chair, that there are certain requirements in the way of formal education which are not, in my humble opinion, likely to be met by sending boys and girls wandering through the village during school hours to buy wood from the joiner and metal from the smith when they should be at their desks learning to do their sums and write a decent piece of English prose.'

'Perhaps,' said the Major, 'the headmaster will enlighten us.' The headmaster was not entirely sure to whom the Major's irony was directed but he began to explain what he meant by a project and its aim — to relate what the children learned in school to life outside and its practicalities. He catalogued the steps involved and the skills required to carry them out: drawing, arithmetic, the calculation of the cost, the determination of the circumference of the wheel and therefore of the steel rim — a calculation, he did not need to remind the Board, that involved the use of the formula $2\pi r$. At this point the parish minister broke in. 'Mr Chairman, this is what I can only call high-faluting nonsense. What need do these children have of formulas? what earthly reason is there for sending girls to a smithy where they may unfortunately be exposed to a good deal of profane language and coarse talk when what they need to know is how to cook a decent meal for their man when he comes in at the end of the day and how to knit a pair of stockings or a jersey for a child?' The rest was liberal nonsense calculated to undermine those traditions of solid learning which had made Scottish education the envy of the civilized world. Yes of the world. No doubt like so much other rubbish such ideas had been imported from the Continent. From Germany, no doubt, where he understood there were those who favoured such experiments in education — or perhaps it was Italy. In any event what was good for the Continent was by no means necessarily good for the bairns of Slateford. He called on the Board to place on record its unequivocal condemnation of the teaching methods adopted by the headmaster, who should remember, though he seemed inclined to forget it, that he was responsible in the first place to the Board. And he would not accept the argument he had heard on a previous occasion that Mr Scott was responsible only to His Majesty's Inspector of Schools. This was a matter for the parish and no one else.

At the use of the word 'liberal' the grocer had bridled. He now intervened to ask — through the chair — whether the speaker was making a political attack on supporters of the Liberal Party of which he was proud to be one. He himself had always considered education to be above and beyond party and would greatly deplore the introduction of politics into the debate. The Major told him not to be daft, adding that this was not for the record, and the parish minister assured the grocer that there was no direct political thrust to his contribution. If he had used the word liberal it was, as it were, with a small 'l'. The grocer declared himself satisfied. The Reverend James Murdoch — significantly as it seemed to the headmaster — was non-committal and said he would wait to hear what the headmaster had to say. As he listened, the headmaster wondered whether the reference to Continental influences was a glancing reference to Elizavyeta; either way it was unimportant. He would stick to sure ground. He began therefore by questioning a view of education that limited it to mere dexterity with numbers and rote learning. And reading and writing, the minister interrupted. And even reading and writing, the headmaster went on raising his voice a little, if they were not seen as tools that could be used in society. It was his view, and he was not alone in this, that education, if it was to be fruitful, must be related to life outside the school, must be perceived by the children to have such a relationship otherwise there would be disciplinary problems and more work for the attendance officer chasing truants. What was education? Was it to be confined to the mechanical reproduction of numbers or the ability to copy a model letter? He felt that it was more justly seen to be the attempt to make children use their minds so that, wherever they were, wherever life called them, they would be able to address their minds to practical problems and, if necessary, use their knowledge of numbers, their ability to write a decent hand and put a page of English together, to solve them. He was proud to quote the saying of a great Scottish writer and philosopher, Thomas Carlyle, who had said that two men he honoured and no third: the first being the man who worked with his hands and the second the thinker. Education must be a bond between those who worked with their hands and those who thought. That was the aim of his educational practice.

Of course, said Elizavyeta, they were bound to be alarmed. Of course the parish minister would say this was dangerous nonsense — remember he was putting into his attack all his resentment at that fact that the Major had quashed the issue of our relationship. Of course your Liberal grocer sat somewhere in the middle along with the Free Church minister. Of course the Major didn't block the proposal to refer the matter to the Education Authority of the County. You are learning the hard way, my dear, but you are learning. If you could pass on to your pupils some of the lessons you have learned in the last year you might make them think differently about their lives and fates here among the hills. Suppose they did refer the matter to the Education Authority; how could that possibly harm him? He would have the Inspector on his side for one thing. If necessary he would have to canvass the members of the Authority and put his case. He would have to fight. So evening after evening he mounted his bicycle and rode off to knock at the doors of farmhouses where the owners listened to him on the doorstep and he despaired of penetrating their prejudices. He rang the bells of lawyers and doctors in little country towns and explained in front parlours to men of set opinions the appropriateness, and, as he saw it, efficacy of his teaching methods. He went eventually to a great house set at the end of a long drive spanned by a memorial arch to the same boy as was commemorated in the village hall. There the owner received him in the library, listened, took notes and then said: 'Mr Scott, your method seems thoroughly sound and well-based. You may count on my support. Whom else have you seen?' He listened to the names and a smile came over his aristocratic face. 'You have some of my tenants in that list. I don't suppose you had much luck. I'll have a word with some of them. Good evening, Mr Scott. I am glad you came.'

Elizavyeta rode out to meet him on the road home. As they cycled towards the village they heard a cuckoo call insistently by the West Water. Among the young hay a corncrake rasped. 'Râle de genêt,' she said with a laugh. They cycled without much discretion up to the villa. In the drawingroom they sat and held hands and talked. How did she explain, he wanted to know, that the big landowner, the aristocrat, was the only one who seemed to understand what he was talking about? How did that square with her talk about class interests? She rebuked him for his crude analysis. The landowner might be a perfectly intelligent man, open to persuasion and willing to support an educational method which — this was something the farmers and the parish minister did not understand — not only did not threaten his interests but could actively further them; for to have young men and women working on his estates who had actually been taught to think meant that from their number he could draw overseers — grieves, they called them, didn't they? — housekeepers and servants who would run things efficiently. But he should mark one thing — the weapon the landowner had indicated he would use to bring the farmers to heel: the threat of a landlord to a tenant. In any case he could relax now. He would probably hear no more of it.

The table was laid in the dining-room as usual for his solitary evening meal. Three weeks had passed. There had been a meeting of the Education Authority but Elizavyeta was right: he had heard no more of the matter. But he was still on his guard, still conscious of a threat, aware that he could count on no real certainty any more. When Miss Grant, his Highland housekeeper, with her mild, slightly startled face, brought in the minced collops that were his supper she laid a letter by his place. A young lady had brought it, she explained, 'She said it was urgent and I was to see you got it right away when you came in.' He waited till she had left the room — she contrived to linger on the pretext that the hearth needed tidying — before he ripped open the envelope. In Elizavyeta's hand with its indefinable foreignness it said: 'Come quickly — as soon as possible. Love E.' He ate hurriedly, refused Miss Grant's rice pudding and rode off, indifferent to who might see his haste or his destination.

At the villa the front door was open and there were trunks in the doorway. Lienchen was carrying travelling rugs down from the bedroom. She said nothing as usual and disappeared down the hall with an uncommunicative glance. Elizavyeta was in the brown coat with the brown hat and veil which he remembered from the first time he saw her at the station. She took his hand and led him into the drawingroom where the furniture was hidden under dustcovers. 'Loved John,' she said. 'I have to leave. At once, today.' He opened his mouth to ask a question but she laid a hand on his lips. 'I shall not come back — or not for a long time — if I come back at all. You are not to wait for me. Boris has escaped. He has got out of Russia and is in Berlin. I must go to him.' He could say nothing but felt a tear run down his face and on to his hand. 'If I can get to Perth I can catch the night-train and be in London tomorrow. The children have gone already. Don't mourn. You mustn't mourn or regret anything. What you must think is that for a time we were close and loving together. That we won something from life.' He had an extraordinary sensation as if his chest had suddenly become hollow. She had taken her hand from his lips but his tongue cleft to the roof of his mouth. 'I must finish the last packing,' she said and left the room. John sat on the dustsheet that covered the sofa and felt the tears well up. His weeping was silent, hot and burning. She came back into the room, walked up behind him and, taking his head in her hands, wiped his tears. 'I want you to keep this,' she said, 'as a keepsake — is that the word?' It was the wooden bird he had noticed on her desk on his first day in the villa, peasant-carved, smooth, solid. He took her in his arms and she laid her face on his chest. 'You mustn't think it isn't hard for me too,' she said, looking up. She was silent for a little. 'There was something my mother always used to say if we went on a journey. She said it was good just to sit on your luggage for a few minutes and think of what you were leaving and where you were going. I think I'll do that now. Listen, the train is in half-an-hour. Will you do something? Will you cycle to the level crossing where I used to walk with the children to watch the train go past so that I can see you from the window? Now I'd like to sit and be alone — on my luggage.'

It was a mile to the level crossing. He was aware that hers was a merciful ploy to fill the time till she left and to make it easier for him and perhaps for herself. To get to the level crossing he had to pass through the woods that lay on the road into the village from the south. He rode quickly, using his gears, feeling the evening air blow through his shirt and dry the tears on his face. When he reached the gates they were still open. He looked at his watch. There were still five minutes before the train left. The level-crossing keeper came out of his house, looked at him curiously and bade him good evening. John responded, then bent down to fiddle with his trouser-clips and went through a pretence of checking the tension of his bicycle-chain. The single hoot of the train leaving the station came across the woods. If he laid his ear to the rail he would be able to hear them ring with the noise of the wheels; it was a game the village children played, one which he had warned them against just as he had spoken against the risk of laying halfpennies on the line in the hope that they would be squashed into pennies. These were the irrelevancies that stirred in his mind as he watched the keeper close the gates and then go back to stand in the door of his house. The track described a bend as it skirted the end of the wood. The engine appeared. Seen from the gates it seemed very high; foreshortening made it look breasted like a pouter pigeon. The carriage window would be high above his head. He saw her brown hat which she held with one hand, the pale outline of her face and her other hand that waved and blew a kiss. Then she withdrew into the carriage. The keeper opened the gates. John remounted his bicycle and rode home.

There is in such moments of separation a feeling of mutilation, as if some part of one's being had been wrenched away leaving a wound that will bleed unstaunchably. It is a pain of the mind or the heart but one that exhausts the victim as if it were a physical trauma. It is inescapable, cannot be thrown off, survives the oblivion of sleep and returns with waking or triumphs in our dreams. People do not ordinarily die of it. Those who kill themselves no doubt do so out of despair, out of the belief that it will never cease, never be assuaged, never diminish. The truth is that it does all these things but not before it has exhausted us, shaken us, brought us to tearless silence. In the process there are moments when we may wish that we had built into us as it were, some self-destruct mechanism in the head or at the nape of the neck, that would operate simply and quickly. The pain can be dulled by work, by new attachments, by a change of place or of interests, but it will well up unexpectedly and fill us suddenly for no apparent reason and at inappropriate moments with a sadness that can neither be shared nor explained. I have a feeling that it may burst out again in our last moments so that death is a welcome escape.

But the interesting and unanswerable question that remains when I think of the parting of John Scott and Elizavyeta de Pass and of the real, deep pain both suffered is to what extent there was buried deep down, deeper than all the springs from which their tears flowed, a tiny seed, a bud or shoot even, of relief, so that on the following Saturday when he cycled into town he could with one part of his being enjoy the warm almost cloudless day. They were cutting the hay on the hillside farms. The barley was long in the ear and soon would turn to brown. The swallows and martins traced their arcs just above the surface of a mill-pond — a sign, they say, of good weather — and drank in their flight. As he cycled home the hills were purple with bell heather. But what he was conscious of above all was a sense of tension relaxed, of pressures removed. He could not admit it yet but there was a sense in which he was already on the way to recovery, a convalescent. For by now he knew, but could not admit it, that he lacked the courage to break loose, to share the unanchored life that Elizavyeta had sketched for him, its vague promise of meeting him (in what circumstances?) as someone of whom she was 'very fond' — knew it not by any cold process of logic but from daydreams, from thoughts on waking whereby he imagined himself in London, in Geneva or in Berlin among strange men and women to whom he felt no ties and who even in his imaginings kept Elizavyeta from him: Elizavyeta whom he recalled with desire and despair, remembering tiny details of her body, a hair growing from the pink corona of a nipple, a little red spot in the fold of her groin, the feel of her hair and the safe, moist warmth of her body when she took him to her. But still she haunted him. At the summer prize-giving, for instance, presided over with extreme condescension by Miss MacIllroy. The school wheelbarrow was wheeled in by Frank Low, its guardian and keeper, and placed in front of the platform. It was a moment — or could have been — one of quiet triumph to enjoy as the children rose to sing *Jerusalem*. He began to sing too but suddenly stopped as he remembered how Elizavyeta had told how she had cycled past and heard them singing some sort of hymn. 'Not a hymn really,' he had replied, 'but a statement of faith — something you would approve of — about how we could make a new heaven and a new earth here in England or Scotland or wherever you like.' 'I will support the new earth,' she replied, 'but I'm not sure about the new heaven.' Then they had walked through the fields to the red castle with its walled garden and its figures, carved in the soft stone, of the liberal arts, the planetary deities, the cardinal virtues. At one point they could read the motto of the family that had built it: *Dum spiro spero*. While I breathe I hope. 'A good motto,' she said, 'let's make it ours.' The singing stopped. Miss MacIllroy stood up to present the prizes. He had to concentrate on the names of the prizewinners. When it was all over he walked through the classrooms before locking the main doors. Already he had accepted that for a year, two years, even more, this would be his world.

It was commented on by Miss Grant and by Mrs Ramsay who were in the habit of exchanging views and information on the subject of a man in whom both had a certain proprietary interest, that when that woman left — a nice enough person no doubt but stuck up and someone that kept herself to herself, although mind you you could see from the way she dressed that she was quite a lady — he had flung himself into gardening, rising up early to clear the stones, sieve the earth, burn the weeds and plant potatoes to clean the soil. They noticed too that he did a fair bit of fishing — not with Willie Hamilton but by himself in hill-burns high up the glen and that he seldom took the road to the West Water past the villa. They had been very thick, he and the lady from the villa, always off on their bicycles — not mind you that anyone could be positive that there had been anything more between them, although Miss Grant hinted that she had her suspicions but was not prepared to substantiate them, for there are some things a person can't say. What they agreed on was that she would never have made a headmaster's wife; she was too stylish for that with airs and graces that were too grand for a schoolhouse. But it was a great waste to see him living alone in that fine, new stone house that just needed a woman to take it in hand, get some decent furniture into it and make a home of the place. There was Miss Troup, a nice lassie and full of spirits, though she was going steady with young Adams of Stracathro, who used to be a bit of a lad but seemed to have simmered down a little. Or there was May Mitchell. She had been sweet on him once and still hankered after him to judge by the way she looked across to his pew when she got down from the organ and took her seat to listen to the sermon. In the autumn Miss Troup announced her engagement to Mr Adams but May still cast looks in John's direction to no avail. It looked as if she'd end up an old maid, said Mrs Ramsay, for she must be twenty-eight if she was a day.

So school resumed. That autumn the headmaster did not argue over the date or the duration of the potato holidays which made the Major comment that the dominie was a bit glum these days and wonder in an amused way to the Reverend James Murdoch whether it had anything to do with the departure of a certain lady; whereupon the minister said that, gossip from some quarters to the contrary, there had never been any evidence to his mind that the friendship between Mr Scott and the lady had ever gone beyond the bounds of propriety, being based on a professional and tutorial arrangement with the children, who, he understood were not hers, but merely lodged with her. The Major commented that there were some great innocents in the world and added that he hadn't thought this solemn-faced headmaster of theirs would have had so much spunk in him. The minister's attitude reflected an attempt, as it were, to reclaim the headmaster for the community which began to lose interest in the subject of the villa and its tenant now that it lay closed and shuttered. The time was propitious, as his wife remarked, to get the headmaster a wife — it was high time he had one and May Mitchell would do very well. It was presumably at Mrs Murdoch's instigation that the minister brought John Scott and the organist together to organize a school choir that would perform at the Christmas party. This he did after the evening service on Sunday, calling them both into the vestry where Willie Hamilton was putting away the pulpit bible and hanging up the minister's gown. There was a moment of awkwardness as the couple stood in front of the minister and waited while Willie Hamilton lingered on brushing the minister's frock coat and black basin-shaped hat. There can be little doubt that through the minds of each person present the thought passed that they looked like a couple seeking advice on matrimony, on the proclamation of the banns and the order of the marriage service. There was, John saw, as the minister broached the idea of the choir to be no escape, no way out; the village was about to claim him as its own. With a certain air of resignation he agreed. Then came the practicalities. He was aware, said the minister, that Miss Troup was an excellent singing teacher but she was to be married shortly, which was a cause of joy to all involved, and there was no guarantee that her successor, when appointed, would be up to the task; so in the general interest of the village and of the children he suggested that May should hold a choir practice once a week after school. Together the pair walked down he aisle and out into the street. 'We had better talk it over,' said May. 'Will you come over on Saturday and have a bite with us? Jim will be pleased to see you. He's decided he wants to go on and study engineering but he'll need some help with his maths. Phemy's at her auntie's in Edinburgh. She's looking for a job in a dress-shop and her auntie's in the business.' She supplied the information flatly but with a sure awareness of what she was about. John looked at the ground for a moment before agreeing.

When he arrived at the mill on the Saturday references to his absence were oblique. 'It's been a while,' said May's mother but did not press the point. There was a great spread of food, May having been the chief cook according to her mother. Jim was on his best behaviour and appeared genuinely interested in knowing how he might get an engineering degree at Glasgow. Mr Mitchell concealed his thoughts and feelings behind his beard as usual, produced a bottle of mead and said: 'You'll have a drop, I hope, but mind ye dinna fa' ower this time.' So continuity was re-established and the hiatus since his last visit obliterated. By the time the wheat was threshed and the tall conical stacks rose in the farmyards above the roofs of the steadings John was once more a regular visitor. There was something soothing in the talk about the mill and quality of that year's wool, in the gossip about the farms round about and who had got the best prices for his yearling wethers at the Trinity Fair, even in Jim's talk about petrol engines, motor cars and motor cycles and the aeroplane that had landed in a field near the Burn estate and how the flier was a friend of Major MacIllroy's, who said the aeroplane would make the next war completely different from any war of the past. 'What next war?' May asked fearfully. 'The one with Germany, of course,' said Jim and added he hoped he'd be old enough to be in it, maybe not flying an aeroplane but at least working on the engines.

May got into the habit of walking John part of the way home — as far as the suspension bridge over the East Water. At first she simply held his hand for a second or two when she wished him goodnight. Then she took his hand most of the way. When he freed it on the pretext that he needed two hands to push his bicycle, she quickly found it again. As they parted she pressed it strongly. After a few weeks they exchanged a brief kiss which John felt as a betrayal of some kind but justified to himself in a moment of jealousy with the reflection that Elizavyeta was no doubt with her husband, Boris, who in turn would no doubt exercise his conjugal rights. On his next visit May announced that she must run up the road to the farm for a jug of buttermilk to make scones and disappeared leaving him alone with her mother. Mrs Mitchell came straight to the point: 'John Scott, what are your intentions with our May. We've been very patient and shut our eyes to some gey funny goings-on, I can tell you. And we're prepared to let bygones be bygones. But I will not have that lassie of mine made a mock of the village and of the whole parish. It's up to you. If you ask my advice you'll be married before the New Year. It's not right a man of your age living by yourself in a fine house with that poor creature, Miss Grant, doing for you. So make up your mind, young man, or else you needna darken our door again.'

It was, I believe, with a certain relief that my father said he understood. So when May came back her mother simply said: 'May, John has something to tell you' and left the room. May put her jug of buttermilk down and ran her hands over her apron with a nervous gesture. 'Well, John, what is it?' He looked at her and was dumb. 'John dear,' she said, 'ye dinna need tae tell me. I guessed it the moment Ma spoke. Oh John, I'll make you happy, you'll see.' She ran up to him and put her arms round his neck; he looked down and was filled with a sense of pity for them both then he lowered his head and placed his lips on her hair. When suppertime arrived Mr Mitchell came in as usual smelling of machine oil and sheep's wool. His wife said May had a surprise for him. He turned his head calmly to the young woman, received her announcement with equanimity, looked round and nodded at John. When they sat down he clasped his hands before him on the table and requested the Lord to make them truly thankful for what they were about to receive. Then he began to eat, chewing slowly and reflectively. There was little conversation during the meal as if everyone were fully occupied with their thoughts. When the women had cleared away and the clatter of dishes from the scullery covered whatever it was they were saying to each other in quick exchanges that were elliptical, practical and devoid of sentiment, Mr Mitchell walked to a seat by the window and said to no one in particular: 'She's not a bad lass, May. It's high time she was wed. I expect you'll do as well as the next one.' Then he folded his hands on his lap and nodded off to sleep.

There were problems about the date of the wedding. To an early date there was the objection that it would look indecently hurried as if — you know what people are like — there was some reason for the haste; in any case the house had to be properly furnished and May's things got together. Christmas was out of the question since it would mean that the couple were away on their honeymoon either over Christmas or New Year or both and thus absent from the family reunion at the mill. So it was fixed for Easter. At the next School Board the headmaster was congratulated on his forthcoming marriage to Miss May Mitchell by the chairman, Major MacIllroy, who — but this was not in the minutes — looked at the headmaster with an ironical smile as he spoke the words. The interim was filled with shopping expeditions as far afield as Dundee and Perth to order furniture, carpets, fittings, china, cutlery, kitchen utensils; for after a brief inspection of the schoolhouse Mrs Mitchell had pronounced it woefully inadequate. John listened to debates on colours, quantities, prices, with a detachment that was not so much boredom as an inability to become engaged. He had the sensation of inhabiting a perfectly transparent capsule, a thin vitreous covering like an egg-shell, through which he observed his future wife, his future mother-in-law, the obsequious salesmen and saleswomen, and heard the congratulations of Mrs Ramsay, Miss Grant and Miss Troup — now Mrs Adams and, said Mrs Ramsay, who had a sharp eye for such matters, already pregnant, adding to Miss Grant's confusion that 'the lassie had liked the ramming well enough, now they'd see how she liked the lambing.' Within his shell he felt perfectly safe and able to think about Elizavyeta while controlling his sorrow, which had turned into something like a long mourning, as if she were dead, and did not exist somewhere, talking, arguing, laughing and lying in bed with her long arms and long legs and her gently sliding breasts, sharing her bed with a man who was presumably circumcised, had a moustache, hair brushed back and a stubborn face. Within his safe space he allowed himself to have fantasies — had them at strange times. Thus one evening on the train back from shopping in Dundee he imagined he had made his way to some foreign capital like the Vienna of the postcard she had sent him the previous summer, found her in a room like the drawingroom where they had parted, struck down the man who sat beside her on the sofa and carried her off. At other times he allowed himself to have memories of touching, of holding and keeping, of laughing and playing, of being one.

In these moments of abstraction May would lean forward

and tap his knee saying: 'John come back.' Then he would shake himself free of his dreams and smile, touching her hand sadly, for he guessed she knew the nature of his thoughts and the reason for his withdrawal. At other times he would look at May — in a railway carriage, at the mill, at choir practice — and wonder what, if anything they would find and explore together, tried to imagine what lay modestly hidden there; then conscious of his gaze she blushed and whispered: 'You mustn't look at me like that. What will people think?' What they thought was that it was about time he settled down after that carry-on with the foreigner; that he had done very well to get engaged to May for there was a pretty penny in the miller's bank account and one day May would get her share of it no doubt; that the schoolhouse was being done up from top to bottom, no expense spared, everything of the best; that there was one thing you could say about Mr Mitchell — he wasn't grippy, at least where his own were concerned. Meanwhile John remained perfectly calm, polite to everyone, indifferent to them all and indeed to everything. It was a state of mind that allowed him to play his part with precision. Besides May, only his mother was fully aware of his retreat into himself as he discovered when they went to visit her on a day-trip. She was on her best behaviour, did not complain unduly, and did not talk about her late husband, offered a meal that was no better and no worse than usual. But every now and then she would look at her son and wonder what was going on behind the transparent partition that separated them. What filled her with a kind of fear mixed with pity was that she recognized in him the look his father had worn throughout most of their life together — after the first miscarriages and the beginning of her long history of obscure and unmentionable ailments. But she knew no way of breaking through to John any more than she had known how to break through to his father. And his brother sensed it, too, when he arrived on the day before the wedding to be best man. 'Come on, John,' he said. 'It's not that bad. You'll have someone to keep you warm at night at least. That's more than I can say. Have a dram.' He pulled a flask from his pocket and poured a couple of whiskies. John thanked him. He was touched by a caring note in his brother's voice and by the admission of loneliness. He recognized, too, Tom's tact in not mentioning Elizavyeta. For a moment he was on the point of talking about her but he shied away from it. The two brothers knew very little of each other. Perhaps that was how life was or had to be. He wondered if it could be borne. Such were his thoughts on his last night alone.

It was, in fact, not his last night alone — or not technically so — for after the wedding they took the train to Perth and so on to London overnight. May was excited and embarrassed by the confetti because people would know. Their wedding night consisted in his partially undressing in the swaying sleeper and clambering up past where May lay in the lower bunk. She had removed he knew not how much of her clothing for she had asked him shyly to go out into the corridor while she got ready for bed. When he was in his bunk a pang of compunction made him lean over and look down. She was awake with the clothes drawn up to her neck and gave a nervous smile. 'Are you all right?' he asked. She said Yes and then wondered, as the train swayed and jolted over the points, whether it was safe. He reassured her and stretched down his arm; cautiously she extended hers until their hands touched. 'Goodnight,' he said. She echoed him. The train gave a long screech and tore into the dark of a tunnel. Next day there was the same avoidance of intimacy: she lay with her back to him as he shaved and dressed, nicking his ear slightly as the train lurched at a junction somewhere. He sat on the edge of her bunk and dabbed at the cut with the towel until the bleeding was staunched. She asked if anything was wrong. He reassured her and went out into the corridor where he watched the telephone wires swoop between the poles, spotted the grade indicators and counted the mile posts. He took out his watch and estimated the speed at over sixty. There was a smell of soot and polished brass. Outside the landscape was tamely flat. A shower sent raindrops chasing each other diagonally across the window. There were barges on a canal where the water dimpled in the rain; a heron rose from a marshy field.

He knocked gently on the door. Her voice asked him to wait a minute. Shortly she came out and stood beside him and took his hand. Weren't they in London yet? Wasn't he excited? She could see that he was locked in his usual calm but her sense of expectancy overcame her. There were a couple of hours yet, he explained. Once they got to London they had to get from Euston to Victoria and catch the boat-train to Dover. When would they be in Paris? That night. How would they get across London? Would they see the Tower? or the Horse Guards? No, he said, smiling a little and putting his hand on her arm, for he was moved by her sense of excitement. On the way back. Was there any confetti on her dress, she asked and turned round for his inspection. He picked a couple of tiny specks off her collar and reassured her. It was almost like travelling with a child, although he was already aware that with her naïveté went a hard-headed sense of reality and the ability to wait for what she had set her mind on. In her determination she took after her mother, who must have had much the same look when the miller fetched her from the Black Isle, where her father farmed a croft and the language of everyday was Gaelic: 'a penniless lass wi' a lang pedigree' she used to say of herself looking back on that day from the security of the mill. May would not be penniless but she was in other respects her mother's daughter.

So their first night was in Paris in a little hotel in the rue du Colisée, near the Etoile; John had used it once before, on his way back from Perpignan. The room gave on to a street where at dusk prostitutes loitered in the doorways. As he looked out May examined the room with its complicated plumbing, its strange washbasin and the odd enamel contraption beside it. What was it? she asked. He replied that the French called it a bidet, which meant a pony. Oh, she said and ventured the guess that it was for washing your feet. Then she unpacked carefully, laying her underwear modestly away in the dressing-table drawers and hanging up her coats and dresses with an air of concentration. At dinner she was anxious lest she should be asked to eat frog's legs and reacted nervously to the attentions of the waiter and the sounds of a strange language. She ate some veal but was uncertain of the sauce which had mushrooms in it. She drank some white wine and wrinkled her nose at the taste. She had an ice which she ate with relish. Then they walked down the Champs Elysées amid the lights, the clatter of cabs and the noise of the taxis. In a café they watched the crowds go past, sauntering, hurrying, idle or purposeful. There were officers with delicately coloured képis and light blue dress uniforms who reminded him of the garrison in Perpignan. There were boys in sailor suits and girls in boots and long skirts; women with dresses they lifted delicately to cross the avenue and avoid the droppings of the cab-horses. Driving past went very grand-looking ladies who, he surmised, were the *poules de luxe* of whom Lebrun used to speak. They greeted each other from their carriages or from the motor cars they rode in daringly, veiled and scarved, behind their chauffeurs. Then they walked slowly back to the hotel. In their bedroom she undressed quickly, modestly, with her back to him and slipped into bed in a long white nightdress with embroidery at the neck and lace at the wrists. He was equally guarded and expeditious. In bed he felt the warmth of her hip where it touched his. She put her hand in his in a trusting way and said; 'It was a long day.' He agreed and reached for the electric light switch. In the dark she curled up a little and moved slightly closer. He lay awake and listened to her breathing become shallower. Then he turned over and fell into the dark pit of sleep. It was not until three nights later that the marriage was consummated. In the night something woke him and he was aware of her naked thigh where the nightdress had ridden up in her sleep. Her warmth and closeness stirred his flesh and he gently turned her on her back. As his hand slid under her nightdress and felt for her breasts she raised a hand for a moment as if to stop him and then surrendered to his explorations. In the morning she was confused and embarrassed at first saying with a laugh: 'I suppose we're really married now.' 'Yes,' he said. 'I suppose so.'

It was not then that I was conceived. Not until three months later on a warm June in the front bedroom of the schoolhouse while the corncrakes were strident in the field beyond the church. In that respect I am the product of heat and insomnia. When in due course the doctor came to examine my mother she ran off upstairs and locked herself in the bedroom. Mrs Mitchell had to coax her down to the drawingroom and the couch on which she reluctantly allowed the ritual to take place. So she told me with a laugh in her old age, with my father dead and the truth about this and other mysteries rising to her pale lips as if some inner censor had been overcome as she waited for her cancer to mature. What she did not describe was the way in which she had waited hopefully each month for her periods to stop, keeping a careful record in her mind and on a calendar in the kitchen where she pricked the dates with a pin so that no one might guess at her calculations, at her impatience for an event which would, she knew, though she feared it, secure her position, provide her with a base from which to confront her husband, the village and that ghost from the past whom she feared and hated.

By the autumn her pregnancy was triumphantly visible. She stood at the window and watched the ploughmen flitting — moving to new farms after the feeing markets when they had walked the pavements of the market towns with braided straw in their lapels to show that they were for hire. Now the high two-wheeled carts were on the move. The man walked at the horse's head or heaved himself up to perch on the shaft of the cart; behind him were piled a table, some chairs, perhaps a wardrobe, covered with a tarpaulin that sheltered not only the sticks of furniture and their other worldly goods but his wife and children as well. A dog ran at heel or padded along underneath the cart, sheltering from the showers that drenched the ploughman and sent rivulets of water down the folds of the tarpaulin under which the children wept and huddled together in the cold. May watched them pass and was grateful that she had a roof over her head and a fire in the grate, a husband who had a good job and maybe prospects of moving to a bigger school in a town. It was much to be thankful for and, in her own silent way, she was thankful and therefore submissive to his silences at table and to the fury of his silent lovemaking. She knew him now, knew how to handle him; just how much she knew she kept to herself and discussed with no one the way he would wake sometimes in a lather of sweat, fighting some dream in which he muttered indistinctly, perhaps in French, and then fell asleep with a sudden sob or a sigh, she was not sure which. The cart had rumbled on up the street and she was turning to go about her housework when she saw the postman come cycling down the road, and, standing on one pedal, freewheel up to her gate. What he delivered was a small, thin oblong parcel bearing unfamiliar stamps. 'Bonny stamps, Mrs Scott,' said the postman and rode off slinging his big red bag behind him. The parcel was addressed to Mr John Scott, the Schoolhouse, Slateford. What the stamps were she did not know. French? There was no word on them that looked like France. Carefully she turned it over. On the back in a strange hand but one she knew must be a woman's was written: Abs: (whatever that might mean) E. de Pass and a complicated address.

She took the parcel into the front room and, laying it on the table, considered it carefully, lifted it and smelt it as if it might still bear the telltale perfume of its sender. But it smelt only of wet brown paper. She lifted it, put it to her ear and shook it. Nothing rattled inside. She ran her fingers along the side of the rectangle. It was not a box yet it was quite stiff. Very gently she tested to see whether it would bend, which it did slightly. She laid it down once more and examined the fastening of fine, tough string; the knot was sealed with blue wax and bore the impress of a signet-ring or coin. She glanced at the clock on the mantelpiece. There was an hour yet till dinnertime. She left the room and shifted a pan on the grate so that the stewed mince would not catch. Then she wiped her hands carefully on the kitchen towel and went back to the front room and the package lying there on the tablecover — a fine blanket from the mill which she had had dyed green to match the chairs and the sofa. She walked round the table. A noise made her start but it was only a bedroom door banging gently in the wind. Then with great speed and decision she went to the cane work-basket by her chair and took out a pair of scissors. Carefully, skilfully, without harming the paper she cut the string and laid it on one side. Then she unfolded the paper and found what lay within: a photograph protected by a double layer of corrugated paper. She opened up the last wrappings and confronted the face that looked at her out of the oval cut in the grey cardboard of the mount. What she saw was the face of a young woman looking obliquely, almost over her left shoulder, at the camera. She wore a blouse — or perhaps it was a dress — buttoned up to the neck with a fine lace collar that rose up almost to the sitter's chin. There was a white flower in a buttonhole just above her breasts. The face itself was oval, the brow accentuated by the way the hair was parted in the middle and swept up and back on either side. The eyebrows were short, very straight, plucked to a firm line. The eyes were dark — might have been brown or dark blue; the nose was long and slightly pointed with delicately shaped nostrils. The mouth was slightly open so that the lips had a blurred appearance, as if she had almost begun to speak. The camera had frozen the breath between her lips. The chin was strong and slightly pointed. The skin white and smooth. But that might be the work of the light and not of nature. There was no letter.

May lifted the photograph and turned it on its face. On the back was something she took to be French, the initial E and a date: August 1913. Once again she raised the photograph to her nose and sniffed. This time it seemed to her that she detected the ghost of a perfume for with an angry gesture she threw it down on the table face up. She stood for a few seconds and stared at the image, at the lips which she felt embodied a sensuality that was as dangerous as the quick intelligence of the eyes. With a sudden angry gesture she crushed the photograph so that it bent through the middle and ran into the kitchen. The grate was closed; when she opened the top the flames flared and licked up the back of the chimney. She put her hand in and dropped the photograph into the heart of the flame. As she withdrew it her bare wrist touched the hot iron. She gave an exclamation and raised the burned spot to her lips. There was a red slanting mark on her skin. She was about to replace the cover of the grate when she remembered the wrapping and the string. She ran through to collect them and dropped them on top of the thin white membrane that was all that remained of the photograph.

When she was serving the mince her husband noticed the burn. She saw his glance and before he could remark on it said: 'It's just a wee burn. I caught it on the grate.' Later that afternoon, when the fire had died down she raked carefully through the ashes and sifted away any trace of paper. My father did not know but that was the moment when she decided that she not only possessed power through the child in her womb but that there were other weapons she might use if need be.

The arrival of the photograph and its destruction set her on a search — it lasted months and was interrupted by her advancing pregnancy, then by my birth and the long exhausting business of breast-feeding: the search for any other trace of Elizavyeta. It led her to a minute investigation of those parts of the house, those items in it, which were her husband's: his tin trunk, his suits in the wardrobe which were examined externally and in the pockets for hairs that were not immediately recognizable as his or her own, his shaving-gear, the drawers of his desk, although she knew that they were intended to be sacrosanct and inviolable. She developed a careful technique that involved noting how articles had lain before she moved them and then laying them out on the floor in the exact configuration they had shown in the drawers. But there was nothing even in that holy of holies except some old notebooks marked French Vocabulary, some postcards of Perpignan showing people dancing a circle-dance in a square, a few unused French stamps and a handful coins which might well have been left over from their honeymoon. Carefully she returned everything as she had found it. As she rose from her knees she saw the oval wooden bowl carved like a bird — a duck perhaps — which stood on the top of the desk and held a mixture of rubber bands and drawing-pins. It was, she knew, of foreign make but John was always vague about it, how he had come by it, where it came from. She felt the cross-hatchings on the wood and the long fern-like incisions which conventionally represented the wings and ran her finger round the inside of the bowl where she could feel the roughness the chisel had left on the wood. She turned it up but there was nothing on the bottom to suggest an origin. Yet she was deeply suspicious of it and furious that proof escaped her that it was a keepsake from the woman she still considered to be her rival.

At last there remained only his books and the collection of Ordnance Survey maps of the county which he had the in-furiating habit of scanning of an evening — planning, or more likely remembering, walks and bicycle rides with that woman who had been free, without children, leisured. She began to work her way through the small library a shelf at a time, taking out each book, shaking them open to see what might be hidden in their pages, and then replacing them strictly in the order in which they had stood. Once a piece of paper floated down but it was nothing: notes of train times and a list of things bought with a careful note of their cost. She left to the last the French books which were bound in tattered yellow paper with loose pages and broken spines. The second one she lifted came apart with a flutter of pages. She had to spend half-an-hour restoring the pages to order. She was almost minded to give up but decided to take down a couple more. One of them was a volume of poetry. This time a postcard slid from between the leaves and planed down to the floor. In her haste to retrieve it she almost slipped on the steps she was using to reach this, the highest shelf. The brown postcard showing a great spired church with an eagle spreadwinged across the steep slope of its roof. The superscription on the back was in several languages, one of them English: the Saint Stephen's Church, Vienna. Addressed to Mr John Scott, c/o Mrs

Ramsay, Glenmoriston, Church Street, Slateford. A short message in what she took to be French and the signature E. de P. As if Mrs Ramsay would not be able to decipher that. She put the book back in its place, folded the stepladder and returned it to its place under the stairs. Then she came back to the front room and very carefully laid the card in the middle of the wide blotter that lay on top of the desk.

When John came back from school just as the evening was closing in, she made no mention of her discovery but went on with making the tea, enquiring how the new teacher who had taken Miss Troup's place was doing, what Miss Kerr was up to. Were there many new children now that the flittings were over and the new ploughmen had moved into their cottages at Dalbog and Stracathro? After tea he worked at the table in the front room. The gas lights over the table left the rest of the room, including the desk, in shadow. She was the first to go to bed. John followed soon after. Perhaps, she thought, he had not seen the card. In the dark he suddenly threw back the bedclothes and grabbed her nightdress. She struggled but he at last pulled it off her. Naked she jumped from the bed and ran whimpering to the next room where no doubt I lay in my cot. He caught her there and forced her on to the bed. So my sister was conceived. Next morning the card was gone. Neither of them ever spoke of the incident but it lay between them for the rest of their lives.

'If children at this early age witness sexual intercourse between adults' wrote Freud, 'they invariably regard the sexual act as a sort of ill-treatment or act of subjugation; they view it, that is, in a sadistic sense.' If I did see, though I do not remember 'seeing', in what other way am I to interpret that silent, desperate struggle on the bed?

It was from this time on that he became what people called 'a great fisher,' by which they meant that, in the season, he was often away, morning or evening, on his bicycle travelling to the lower reaches of the Esk where the grilse came running in from the sea, leaping in the deep pools to free themselves of the sea-lice. In the dusk of the evening or the grey of the early

morning he waded patiently up to his thighs in the cold water
and skilfully, cunningly, played the fish till they tired and let
themselves be taken in the net with which he lifted them from
the water with only an occasional thump of the tail. His wife
complained that she was tired to death of cleaning salmon,
sea-trout or brown trout, and tired of eating it too, although
he found ways of disposing of much of his catch; half a salmon
for the Reverend James Murdoch, a salmon steak for Mrs
Ramsay, a couple of sea-trout for the grocer, and even on one
occasion — in a gesture of ambiguous generosity — a whole
salmon, red with blood and creamy between the flakes of the
flesh, to the Major at the Burn. Practically his fishing meant
that he would leave home just after tea and come to bed late,
when the whole house was sleeping, or else rise early and meet
Willie Hamilton in the High Street before riding off with him
to where the water seemed likely to be best that day. As they
rode along they discussed flies and casts and the virtues of
minnows, real or artificial, for bait, but these exchanges were
soon completed and for the rest of their journey he had to
endure Willie Hamilton's reminiscences of South Africa and
the strange freedom war and the army had offered: escape
from the village, from the threat of domesticity, from life at
the tail of the plough. When Willie came home at last it had
been as a middle-aged bachelor with a repertory of stories
hinging on sexual encounters, often with black women of
immense size and unimaginable erotic power, about the
brothels of the Cape and the terrors of the short-arm parades
where the MO paraded the troops to diagnose VD — a
diagnosis followed by confinement to barracks and loss of pay
until the excruciating cure was completed. Willie laughed in
retrospect and wiped his bleary red eyes. He was not so wild
these days, he would add, and then go on to reflect that — you
could take his word for it — there was more went on in
Slateford than met the eye; the barmaid at the Central Hotel,
for instance, was maybe not as shy as she let on. Indeed he had
it on good authority that she was 'a good mow'. All of which I
expect my father let wash over him turning over in his mind a

piece of poetry he was committing to memory — a passage from *The Prelude*, for instance, that spoke of 'a people risen up fresh as the morning star' and declared:

> Bliss was it in that dawn to be alive,
> But to be young was very Heaven!

It was a passage he had only recently discovered; might have shared with Elizavyeta but now could share with no one; for who in Slateford would be interested in how a poet had experienced a political moment of the French Revolution?

From this time, too, dates my father's fame as a gardener whose flower beds under the south gable of the schoolhouse were something people stopped to comment on as they passed on a Sunday morning and summer visitors to the village, finding him digging, weeding, planting, transplanting would enter into conversation about plants and fertilisers. From these labours came the delphiniums, and sweet-peas in summer, the daffodils and lilies in the spring, which my mother bore in armfuls to the church when it was her turn to provide flowers. If my father distributed the fish he caught, my mother distributed the flowers in a way that some people — including Mrs Ramsay — found condescending and in the manner of Lady Bountiful. Perhaps they did not suspect that her display, her generosity with cut flowers and, in their season, with fruit and vegetables, was a cover for her sour awareness that what made her husband rise, when the dawn chorus began, to labour in the garden was his unwillingness to stay in her bed a moment after the light had wakened him and that his fishing expeditions derived from the same motives. She herself was caught up in the business of child-minding and of her second pregnancy and often she had to fight her weakness and fatigue; nevertheless she developed a household regime that was pitiless in its rigour and relentless in its application. It is not difficult to detect an element of revenge in the rule that her husband (and myself in due course) must take off his gardening or fishing boots at the back-door — rain or shine — before entering the scullery: a rule which was extended to his walking shoes which had to be exchanged for soft slippers at the front-door so as not to mar the polish of the linoleum in the lobby. Her regime decreed that the other front room — the drawingroom — where the furniture was normally shrouded in dust-covers, should be used only when there were visitors: the committee of the Women's Guild come to discuss the annual bazaar and to sit sipping tea with their veils pulled up over their noses, which I found comic to a degree and was whipped for commenting on, or Miss Kerr and Miss Stewart (Miss Troup's successor), who were received once a year with regal condescension, or more important still, the minister's wife and the wives of some of the summer visitors, come to the village for the long summer holidays. By the time that I was conscious of the oddity of such matters it had become a drill that not only I but my father had to show our hands to prove they were clean before we sat down to a meal.

Music alone tempered the rigour of my mother's regime. At the onset of her first pregnancy — with me — she had stopped playing the organ in the kirk, but at home there was an upright rosewood piano, a wedding present from her parents, on which she played pieces from what had been her Sunday repertory. So through my childhood there ran certain melodies like Handel's *Largo, Sheep may safely graze,* and Schumann's *Liebestraum,* which — all linguistic evidence to the contrary — was not considered a secular piece. She sang too in a warm contralto psalms and paraphrases and, in a kind of emotional conspiracy, my favourite hymn about the child Samuel in the temple and how the Lord called to him in his sleep: 'Hushed was the evening hymn'/The temple court was dark,/The lamp was burning dim/Before the sacred ark'. Then she would tell me how Hannah, the mother of Samuel, dedicated her son to the service of the Temple — 'for as long as he liveth he shall be lent to the Lord' — and how she made a little coat for him and brought it to him from year to year. Then she would break off and hug me to her with a burst of tears. The hymn, the story and my mother's outburst filled me with a mixture of fear and excitement. She would remind me of that hymn years later

174

when I took a degree, but not in divinity, and failed to fulfill her inward dedication of my life. Other moments were less clouded with emotion. Then I would stand by her music stool and watch the play of the keys; sometimes she would even remove the front of the piano so that I might see the hammers, feel the resonance of the strings and how her voice blended with them. Then she left her church music for what she called 'the auld Scots songs' — *Jock o'Hazeldean, My love is like a red, red rose, The Eriskay Love Lilt* — and we shared a quiet happiness. When I was nine or ten we got a gramophone — the first in the village. There were few records. I do not know on what principle they were chosen. Or by whom. People were invited to hear them, including Willie Hamilton who listened stolidly while John MacCormack sang in a curiously thin voice (the fault no doubt of the recording or the reproduction) *Là ci darem la mano*. It was, he observed as he left, a grand thing — music. My own favourite was *Casta diva* in which Anita Galli-Curci's coloratura acrobatics induced in me a feeling of excitement that verged on the sexual. But my mother's choice was Sullivan's *Lost Chord*: 'Seated one day at the organ/I was weary and ill at ease/And my fingers wandered idly/Over the noisy keys. . .'. She played it obsessively till the record was worn and scratched. The days when she did so were bad days for all of us. I am not sure, looking back, whether the music fed her grief or assuaged it.

Yet in spite of her grief, her fatigue and her gauntness — she looked, her mother declared, like one of the Pharaoh's lean kine — there was clearly some intercourse, including sexual intercourse, between them, for two or three years after my sister's birth there was what I now recognize as another pregnancy, ending presumably in a miscarriage, following which she was in bed for several days. When she got up she dragged herself about the house looking white and drawn so that my sister and I were persuaded she was about to die. Paradoxically perhaps, the thought frightened us very much and led me to interrogate Miss Grant, who had been called in to help in the house, about the prospects of our being partially orphaned. Miss Grant indicated that the matter was in the hands of the Lord, who knew better than we how our lives were shaped. She could only advise us to be good bairns and to pray to Jesus that our mother might be spared. For a little time I interpreted the fact that she did not in fact die to be proof of the efficacy of prayer, but my certainty was challenged by the fact that my pet hedgehog, which was also ailing, did not survive in spite of prolonged supplications to the Lord. Thereafter there were, to my knowledge at least, no further pregnancies. One night when I was ten she came running naked into my bed in what, even at that time and in my innocence, struck me as an attempt to escape from her husband who appeared for a moment in the bedroom door and then disappeared, banging it behind him. From that moment, I believe, I can date that estrangement between my father and myself which lasted for many years and turned in the course of time into a coldness, something approaching hate.

When I was almost a year old — in the summer, that is, of 1914 — my father was cycling back from fishing the West Water when the sun was still visible just north of west and the light, slanting in the late evening through the alders at the water's edge, cast long shadows on the still, clear pools. He looked up — as he always did when passing the villa on the edge of the village — and saw with a start that there were lights in the downstairs rooms. Since Elizavyeta had left it had stood deserted. Rumour in the village had it that the tenant was some foreign gentleman who must have a penny or two to keep a house and not live in it. He made no mention of his discovery to his wife but waited to see how long the intelligence would take to reach her and in what form. By dinnertime next day he sensed at once that she had been informed. She broached the subject without preamble. 'She's back,' she said. 'Who?' he asked with badly feigned ignorance. 'Fine you know — that Miss de Pass.' There was a plenitude of scorn in the 'miss'. 'With a man, if you please. At least there'll be no call for you to go tutoring. There are no children with them this time.' Was it Boris he wondered with his stubborn face back from Siberia, or Paul come to Scotland from Vienna or Berlin or wherever she had spent the years since he last saw her? He said nothing but went on breaking his bread into his broth.

I wish it were probable that somehow he contrived to see her, talk to her, find out what life had done to and with her. But I doubt it. More likely is that one day, walking with his wife and the baby in its pram, he saw her on the other side of the High Street with a man — not a young man with a moustache and fierce eyes but a man in his sixties with a short pointed beard and an elegant walking-stick. She had her hand in his arm and was looking up into his face, talking with the vivacity he remembered. Her hat was small and perched on her head, her coat had the style and the cut which marked her way of dressing. He recognized with a certain excitement the way she held her purse and the gesture with which she tossed the tail of her fox-fur over her shoulder. He almost paused for a second and faltered in his step. Elizavyeta saw him too and, taking her hand from her companion's arm made a gesture of recognition, the hint of a greeting, but his wife tugged at his arm and he contented himself with raising his hat, whereupon the gentleman with the beard raised his too then bent down to his companion as if asking a question. She looked up into his face and answered as they walked on. My mother made no comment. My father knew he had been guilty of a special kind of cowardice and treachery. He took the knowledge of that guilt into his silence.

I believe that when Elizavyeta left Slateford that summer evening two years before it was to meet Boris in Berlin. Their reunion was followed by a period during which their relationship was strained, as is perhaps to be expected when two people who have lived very differently, apart from each other, for a number of years attempt to bridge the gap time and distance have opened. On either side there were thoughts, experiences, memories which both found it hard, if not impossible, to share. They discovered no doubt that physical reunion, in the most basic sense of the term, does not in the long, or even in the short run overcome the gulf of separation.

From Berlin they moved to Vienna, where she at first made allowances for Boris's behaviour because of her understanding of, or her guesses at, the life he had led in the prison camps and then in exile in some hole of a village with no one to talk to except suspicious peasants and an overbearing police official, so that the choice lay between the comforts of the bottle or the embraces of a servant-girl who giggled as she entered his bed. She was called Pelasgaya and smelt of wood-smoke and the cowshed. Sometimes he wondered what had become of the son she bore him, who would in time grow up to be a peasant, sleeping on the top of the stove and uncovering his head before the village headman and the village priest with his beard and vodka-laden breath. He had left her money and intended to send more but gradually he forgot, as he forgot other elaborate plans to fetch the child and bring him up as his own. None of this Elizavyeta resented. They had on that score an understanding that included truthful accounts — not necessarily full ones — of relationships they had entered into with others. So, sitting in a café under the big wheel in the Prater, he heard of her relationship with Paul and with John Scott. The former he found plausible and sensible, but that she should have been involved with a country schoolmaster in Scotland he declared to be not up to her standards. She did not argue but merely said she found it difficult to categorize human beings in that way. His contempt did not disturb her excessively; it was, she felt, a reflection of the general bitterness that stemmed from his experience of prison and exile, a sense of time wasted.

A few days after she had told him about John they met in a café on the Ringstrasse with three friends from St Petersburg; a woman who had worn away her youth and spirits 'going towards the people', the peasants who had rejected her and her companions, stoned them and all but killed them, and two men who wished to sound Boris out to find where exactly he stood politically — more precisely, whether he sided with the Bolsheviks or the Mensheviks. There was, she felt, a curious mismatch between the topics they discussed — his attitude to the possibility of a war between the great imperialist powers, his views on the use of terrorism to raise funds for the revolutionary movement, his opinions about the exact role of a party newspaper, his feelings about the virtues or drawbacks of democratic centralism — and the setting in which the discussion took place with ladies coming and going, Hungarian officers with their pelisses and green trousers parading on the pavement, the servility of the waiters as they brought coffee and cakes. But she was aware, too, that life is full of such contradictions which can pull people apart, tear individuals down the middle, through the heart and brain, unless like the trio from St Petersburg they were totally determined, totally able to abstract themselves from the petty dilemmas of everyday life. She was not sure, she reflected, as she listened to the discussion go to and fro that Boris was of such a heroic mould — which did not mean that she undervalued his anger at injustice and his willingness to act in support of his views — merely that she was aware, indeed was sure, felt it more stongly every day she lived with him, that his politics were based on an impatience which, if frustrated, would lead him into adventures where he would see himself as some sort of avenging angel inflicting retribution for what he and others had suffered. If the revolution demanded terror, he would be its chosen instrument; but he would have little patience for or skill at the long grinding struggle of the factions, for the patient work of a clandestine revolutionary or the difficult tasks of persuasion. His patience, she knew, was paper-thin but she saw with some surprise that he contained himself under their questioning, arguing his points, conceding some things, standing pat on others. The examining commission declared themselves satisfied.

Then they turned to her and asked what she had been doing. Before she could answer Boris replied for her: 'Having an affair with a petty-bourgeois teacher in the Highlands of Scotland.' She rose without a word and walked off. He made no attempt to follow her. That night when he came back to their hotel room he had been drinking. She was silent. Her silence goaded him so that he struck her. She made no sound but took down her suitcase and began to pack unhurriedly, methodically. Next day she was in Munich where Paul was understanding, kind, undemanding. The children welcomed her. So she stayed. Her relationship with Paul was one that allowed tenderness, respect and occasional sexual closeness but no love, no passion. She accepted the relationship on its limited terms, wondering sometimes what would become of her in this difficult world where she had no home, no family, no absolute commitment to a party to sustain her. Paul's business took him to London. She went with him. In London he decided to go on to Glasgow where his lawyer discussed the villa in Slateford and what should be done about the lease. Paul suggested to her that they visit it together. Then she told him about John Scott. It was typical of Paul's tact that he offered to cancel the trip but she said things would not be difficult; they would all meet and no doubt be friends, able to talk about many things. Some friendships, she said, survive separation and remain alive because there is a basis of human trust and liking that endures beyond changes in situations, of living arrangements. She had written to John a couple of times but there had been no reply; which, she thought, meant that his answers had gone astray, been misdirected, not forwarded from one hotel to another as they moved to match Boris's restlessness.

On their second day in Slateford she proposed that they walk through the village and on their way back leave word at the schoolhouse that they would like to have the chance to meet the headmaster. It was on their way up the High Street that she recognized John on the other side of the street with a woman at his side wheeling a pram. With an impulse of pleasure Elizavyeta took her hand from Paul's arm and made a gesture of recognition. John's cold salute in return was like a blow in the face. When Paul bent down to ask if that was the teacher she nodded her head. Tears rolled silently down her face. Paul put her hand under his arm and patted it. They left next day. The villa was once more empty, untenanted. That was in June. Six weeks later there was war.

My father was not called up. He presented himself but was turned down on the grounds that he had a heart murmur. So for him the route of escape under the cloak of patriotism was barred. Even the Rev. James Murdoch went off to France to serve as padre at a base hospital neat Etaples. When he came back he was noticeably less exuberant, presumably because of his stint as officiating minister at the burial parties which continued day after day, two or three times a day, as the dead were collected and laid in their temporary graves. What my father did for the war was to dig up the lawn at the side of the schoolhouse and plant it with potatoes. Walking home up Church Street one dark night in 1916, he walked into a lamp-post and was found unconscious by Willie Hamilton. He was left with a scar on his forehead. After his brother's death in Flanders he retreated further into his silence. His wife was busy in the Red Cross, learning first aid and knitting comforts for the troops: mittens, balaclavas, scarves, socks, or gathering sphagnum moss for dressings. One night a Zeppelin came droning across the North Sea and dropped some bombs in a field a couple of miles from the village. When the war ended there were bonfires.

They are among my clearest memories of the Great War of 1914–1918. Others include strange men in rough uniforms who gave me presents of cap-badges of Scottish, Australian and Canadian regiments; looking through a fence at a long line of horses in an army remount station during a visit to my grandmother in Stirling; and being lifted into the cockpit of a fighter plane when it was unloaded from a railway wagon at Slateford station. But clearest of all is the bonfire on the Muir to celebrate the Armistice, piled high with packing-cases and boxes from the grocer's, with old blinds, dry broom and branches from dead trees. There were cries of 'Burn the Kaiser' and I imagined I saw in the heart of the fire the face of the German Emperor with its fierce upswept moustaches.

As for Elizavyeta, it would be plausible on the basis of some commonsense suppositions to imagine that the history of her war years included refuge in neutral Switzerland, subsidized by Paul, who would be able to go back and forth easily because of his business connections. Boris would appear and disappear a couple of times and finally be caught up, swept away in the Russian Revolution of 1917. Then would come her return to Germany after the War — to Berlin where she would establish herself as the central figure of a number of interlocking groups which were politically and aesthetically radical. Continuing to rely in a friendly way on Paul, she would lead a free, independent life until the Nazi persecution of radicals, intellectuals and Jews — she belonged to all three categories — drove her into exile.

That would be close enough but not quite accurate.

Elizavyeta Mueller-Potapova arrived in Britain as a refugee from Vienna in 1938. The Aliens Office noted of her that she was the wife of Otto Mueller (deceased) and that she had a daughter, Sonya, aged 11. Her address was given as 148 Abbey Road, West Hampstead. She was not politically active. What the official report did not say — presumably because she did not tell them — was that the deceased husband, Otto Mueller, had been a member of the USPD, the left-wing Communist Party; that he had been arrested and imprisoned on the night of the Reichstag Fire; that he had been interned in Dachau and summarily shot there in 1936.

She made a living with some difficulty on the edge of the *schmatter* business — keeping books and typing, dealing with the intricacies of clothes rationing, buying and selling a little here and there on the black market. She kept resolutely distant from politics, as did the other members of the circle of ladies who met in a café near Finchley Road tube station to discuss their children, their marriages, the curiosities of the British character and the stratagems that enabled them to live on the margins of the society that gave them indifferent shelter. After the war, conversation was enlarged to include how to claim for reparations from the German government, the abilities of various international lawyers specializing in such claims, the advisability or otherwise of emigrating once more — to Israel, schemes for the spending of the money when it at last was paid into the bank.

Elizavyeta Mueller used hers to acquire a tiny flat in a large block, the Swiss Cottage exterior of which concealed cramped quarters and long depressing corridors. The other inmates were refugees, pensioners, homosexual bachelors, business girls and a sprinkling of discreet prostitutes. She acquired British citizenship and her interest in politics awoke once more so that in the fifties and sixties she drew to her flat young people on the Left: a radical publisher, the editor of a Marxist journal, members of various Trotskyist groups, young women who typed for her, answered her mail and worked on the papers which might one day be the material for her memoirs. What drew them to her was her spirit, her interest in life, her unhysterical reaction to the behaviour of young people, to their dress, their music and their explosions of unfocused anger and her experience of Russian and German politics, her memories of a heroic age. There was always in her comments on the present a clear dialectical process at work, a sharpness and a practicality that deflated the arguments of revolutionary utopians and cut through the verbiage of fashionable theory.

It was her custom — perhaps her policy — to keep her circle of acquaintances apart; but the intellectual world of the Left is small and sooner or later they met at meetings, conferences, rallies or in senior common rooms, and exchanged notes. One young historian discovered that her first husband, Boris Potapov, had been a friend and protégé of Dzerzhinsky, the founder of the Cheka. It seemed probable that Boris had been a member of that repressive organ of the Revolution. He was liquidated some time in the thirties in one of Stalin's purges. It was one of the women researchers on the other hand, who established that Sonya, who had gone back to Germany shortly after the war, was the daughter not of Mueller but of Boris. There was a photograph of her on her mother's desk but it was never referred to. One day, however, someone asked how it was that the children of men and women who had given their total energies and even their lives to the Revolution were so firm in their rejection of politics. What about Sonya? Suddenly Frau Mueller got up and rummaged in her desk for a cutting from a German illustrated weekly. It was dated 1968. The article was an interview with a German actress who talked of her family, of her husband, a television producer, and of their student son who 'thank God does not have long hair and think his parents are authoritarian'. She put the cutting back in her desk without comment and changed the subject. Then there was the occasion when she was asked about Parvus, the Socialist industrialist who had been close to many of the Russian exiles before 1914 but, after voting for war credits in the Reichstag in that year with the rest of the Social Democrats, proceeded to make huge sums out of government commissions. To her mind the fact that later he was involved in the complicated and obscure negotiations that in 1917 sent Lenin off across Germany in a sealed train on the first stages of a journey that ended in Finland Station in Petrograd did not expunge that fault. But there were others like him, she said. 'I had a friend,' she went on, 'of whom I was very fond and to whom I owe very much. He supported me in some very difficult times. When I knew him first he was a good socialist even if he was an industrialist — after all Engels was one too. Then the war came — the one people used to call the Great War — and I saw how he was swallowed up in the swamp. He was pulled down by the excitement of speculation. Business deals that took him back and forwards to Switzerland. In the end I lost all respect for him although I know he was really a victim of the logic of capitalism and the profit motive. You won't find his name in the history books. It was Paul Schneider.'

She died of cancer in a nursing home in West Hampstead in 1975. The members of her circle of visitors and the few survivors of the coffee and cake sessions in the Finchley Road attended her funeral at Golders Green crematorium. She would have approved, they felt, of the red roses and carnations on the coffin and the record that began to play as it slid out of sight: the joyous pounding revolutionary rhythms of Beethoven's Seventh Symphony.

I do not imagine that her papers — they ended up in the archives of a red–brick university — contained anything that would cast light on the months she spent in Slateford. I doubt that my father's name occurs in them anywhere. She kept no copies of correspondence so there would be no trace of a letter which my mother might have found had she looked further — in the binding of a book, under a drawer in her husband's desk, perhaps even outside in the garden shed in a fine cocoon of cobwebs: the long letter Elizavyeta de Pass wrote shortly after she left on her hurried journey. I believe it might have read like this:

My dear John
I am writing to you from Prague. Accommodation is difficult to get here at least at a price I can afford. I have been lucky and found a small room in a cheap pension. I do not know how long I shall be here. There has been an important conference and I have met a lot of people I have not seen for a long time. My husband, Boris, was also here but he has left again. I do not know where I shall go next. Some people are planning to go on to meet in Cracow in Polish Galicia. They tell me it is a very beautiful medieval town but it can hardly be as beautiful as this great baroque city which one day, we hope, will be the capital of an independent state.

I have been thinking about you a great deal. You know I am very fond of you and so I feel I can be open and frank in what I write. In the short time we knew each other we have been close in a number of ways. You know what I mean by that. I have to admit that I did not expect to find a teacher in the wilds (!) of

185

Scotland with whom I could talk about so many things that interest me and share so much.

I think you are capable of a great deal in life. You are intelligent. You have started to think and to question some of the assumptions of your culture and your class. What I do not know is how far you are prepared to go. In the long run it will not be enough for you to fight and even win little battles with little people on your School Board. You will have to challenge the powers that be — as you call them — more thoroughly. That means politically. Perhaps you should move to some place where you will be able to find people who think like you — people with whom you can grow and develop. The Labour movement is expanding in your country although it is still very backward compared with Germany or Austria or even Russia (although I think Russia is a special case). If you got a post in Glasgow or some other industrial town you could enter politics. You could become a member of Parliament. Why not? I think that in a country like Britain bourgeois democracy should be exploited to the full to achieve socialism.

At other times I think you should have the courage to follow your brother to London. I know you do not think highly of your brother. I believe you are wrong. He has a certain adventurous side to his character which I respect. You have a University degree, which he does not have. You speak French well. There must be some way in a great capital city for you to use your skills and knowledge. You could find some job that allowed you to study, to think and grow intellectually. Indeed why should you not be braver still and move to the Continent, as you English (and Scottish) insist on calling it. You could teach English — with a funny accent — but that would not matter. That is what I would like above all, for it would be easier for us to see each other. For I take it we shall still be good friends. I should like to show you Vienna or Prague or Cracow. You would grow and expand in such places. You would meet men and women who will, I believe, bring about great changes in Europe. Perhaps even in England.

My question is: Do you really have the courage to consider

my proposals seriously? It is not a question of bravery in the way that a soldier is brave. Very stupid people can be brave. So can very reactionary ones. I am talking about the kind of bravery that allows us to break free from the chains that society, class and education have imposed on us. To break free is a great effort. I know how great. All sorts of things keep us prisoner and we have to fight 'in conditions not of our own making' — Who says that? Marx or Engels? There is property, for instance. You live in a nice schoolhouse. Soon you will have planned the garden. Then you will sow seeds. You will plant hedges so that you can sit in the sun where no one can see you and look at your flowers and vegetables and fruit trees. It will be very difficult for you to leave all that *unless you leave soon*. Once the hedges have grown it will be too late. No doubt you will get married and have children. There will be great pressure from many people for you to settle down. Then it will be impossible for you to leave without an even greater effort and there will be pain for other human beings if you do try to escape. You ought to think about these things *now* while there is still time and make a clear and principled decision.

Because there is an alternative. It is that you do not make a clear decision. That you drift into marriage and become a pillar of society, as Ibsen calls them. If you refuse to make a decision that will itself be a decision, though it will not feel like one to you. But I have to warn you — and I do it lovingly — that you will have to pay a price. It is that you will not grow but get smaller. That is not the right word but you know what I mean. You will have your books. You will read French novels and you will learn whole speeches from Racine by heart. You will no doubt have a wonderful garden and people will come to look at your flowers. But what frightens me is that something in you will die. Because if we do not go on growing then something dies inside us. In our minds and hearts. For you there will be no alternative to a death of the spirit. No doubt you will have reservations about society and about religion and about the educational system, but you will keep them to yourself. *In petto*, the Catholics say. You will be a willing prisoner. I have known a number of people who have been in prison. Do you remember the photograph of the woman in my study? She is in prison today but she is fighting from inside her prison and she will never be broken. Have you the will to fight and live? I ask you because I have strong feelings for you and it would hurt me to think you had become a prisoner — if you were to die inside yourself. Forgive me for writing with such frankness. I am used to people who are equally frank with me. Remember always that I am very fond of you.

    Je t'embrasse.

          Elizavyeta.

The imagined past reflects the lived present.

The world's greatest novelists now available in paperback from Grafton Books

Angus Wilson

Such Darling Dodos	£1.50	☐
Late Call	£1.95	☐
The Wrong Set	£1.95	☐
For Whom the Cloche Tolls	£2.95	☐
A Bit Off the Map	£1.50	☐
As If By Magic	£2.50	☐
Hemlock and After	£1.50	☐
No Laughing Matter	£1.95	☐
The Old Men at the Zoo	£1.95	☐
The Middle Age of Mrs Eliot	£1.95	☐
Setting the World on Fire	£1.95	☐
Anglo-Saxon Attitudes	£2.95	☐
The Strange Ride of Rudyard Kipling (non-fiction)	£1.95	☐
The World of Charles Dickens (non-fiction)	£3.95	☐

John Fowles

The Ebony Tower	£2.50	☐
The Collector	£1.95	☐
The French Lieutenant's Woman	£2.50	☐
The Magus	£2.95	☐
Daniel Martin	£3.95	☐
Mantissa	£2.50	☐
The Aristos (non-fiction)	£2.50	☐

Brian Moore

The Lonely Passion of Judith Hearne	£2.50	☐
I am Mary Dunne	£1.50	☐
Catholics	£2.50	☐
Fergus	£2.50	☐
The Temptation of Eileen Hughes	£1.50	☐
The Feast of Lupercal	£1.50	☐
Cold Heaven	£2.50	☐

To order direct from the publisher just tick the titles you want
and fill in the order form.

GF581

The world's greatest novelists now available in paperback from Grafton Books

J B Priestley

Angel Pavement	£2.50	☐
Saturn Over the Water	£1.95	☐
Lost Empires	£2.95	☐
The Shapes of Sleep	£1.75	☐
The Good Companions	£3.50	☐

Alan Sillitoe

The Loneliness of the Long Distance Runner	£2.50	☐
Saturday Night and Sunday Morning	£1.95	☐
Down from the Hill	£2.50	☐
The Ragman's Daughter	£2.50	☐
The Second Chance	£1.50	☐
Her Victory	£2.50	☐
The Lost Flying Boat	£1.95	☐
The General	£2.50	☐
The Storyteller	£2.50	☐
Key to the Door	£2.95	☐
A Start in Life	£2.95	☐
The Death of William Posters	£2.50	☐
A Tree on Fire	£2.95	☐
Men, Women and Children	£2.50	☐
The Widower's Son	£2.95	☐
The Flame of Life	£2.95	☐
Guzman go Home	£2.50	☐
Travels in Nihilon	£2.95	☐

To order direct from the publisher just tick the titles you want and fill in the order form.   GF581A

The world's greatest novelists now available in paperback from Grafton Books

Gore Vidal
The American Quartet

Lincoln	£3.95	☐
Washington DC	£2.50	☐
Burr	£2.95	☐
1876	£2.95	☐

Other Titles

A Thirsty Evil	£1.50	☐
The Judgement of Paris	£2.50	☐
Two Sisters	£1.25	☐
Myron	£1.95	☐
Myra Breckinridge	£2.50	☐
Messiah	£2.50	☐
Williwaw	£2.50	☐
Kalki	£2.50	☐
A Search for the King	£1.25	☐
Dark Green, Bright Red	£1.25	☐
In A Yellow Wood	£1.25	☐
On Our Own Now (Collected Essays 1952–1972)	£1.50	☐
Matters of Fact and of Fiction (Essays 1973–1976)	£1.50	☐
Pink Triangle & Yellow Star	£1.95	☐
Creation	£2.95	☐
Duluth	£1.95	☐

To order direct from the publisher just tick the titles you want and fill in the order form.

GF681

All these books are available at your local bookshop or newsagent, or can be ordered direct from the publisher.

To order direct from the publishers just tick the titles you want and fill in the form below.

Name _____

Address _____

_____

Send to:
Paladin Cash Sales
PO Box 11, Falmouth, Cornwall TR10 9EN.

Please enclose remittance to the value of the cover price plus:

UK 60p for the first book, 25p for the second book plus 15p per copy for each additional book ordered to a maximum charge of £1.90.

BFPO 60p for the first book, 25p for the second book plus 15p per copy for the next 7 books, thereafter 9p per book.

Overseas including Eire £1.25 for the first book, 75p for second book and 28p for each additional book.